One Revolution:

A Year of Flash Fiction

By

Jamie Lackey

Cover by Lukáš Zídka

ISBN
978-0-578-10252-8

Dedications

To Paul, because I couldn't ask for a better husband. I love you.

And special thanks to all of my Kickstarter backers:

Zach Bertrand

Kathryn Board

Pete Butler

John Crandall

Adam Davis

Dan and Emily Hall

Michelle Hilton

Savannah Klunder

Tracey Levino

Cory Livingston

Samuel Montgomery-Blinn

Julie and Jerry Mulligan

Steve Ramey

Jenn Scott

Lois Stefko

Balendra Sutharshan

Linda Vorp

Jeremy Zimmerman

Michael Brendan

Victoria Boardley

Alexis Covato

Brian Creasy

Nathan Griffith

Deanna Hardin

Suzanne Huffman

Don and Debbie Lackey

Aaron Light

Linda McNair

Bill Moran

Ross Pollock

Betsy Scarbro

Jason Strawsburg

Michael Slaysman

Nick and Amy Treadwell

Richard Zapp

Joe and Sabrina Zitzberger

Table of Contents

Introduction

This is my first short story collection. I'm very excited to share it with you. I've been working on it for almost a year now, and it's nice to see that the end is in sight.

One Revolution is the result of my first successful Kicskstarter project, and I'm grateful to everyone who supported me. I've had a lot of fun writing these stories, and this book wouldn't have been possible without the funding I received.

If you're not familiar with it, Kickstarter is an online platform for crowd funding creative projects. It's definitely worth checking out.

This has turned out to be a pretty personal book. Most of the story prompts came from people that I love—from my friends and family. So the stories are colored both by their requested themes and by my relationship with each person.

I'm lucky to have so many wonderful people in my life. Just like **One Revolution**, I wouldn't really exist without their support. Thanks again, everyone.

I hope you enjoy the stories.

A Beltane Dance

April 2012

For Marilla

Cory Livingston wanted me to write him a Celtic story about dancing and love. This was the very first story to go up on my website, and I was so nervous. But then Cory sent me the most wonderful email. He loved it, and he made me feel like the whole project was worth all the nerves, time, and work.

Cathair piled wood on his lonely Beltane fire. At home, everyone would be drinking and dancing, celebrating the spring. His heart ached. Fial was dead, and Cathair was exiled, but time moved on without them.

The accusation of fratricide, falling from Neasa's lips, had wounded Cathair's heart almost as much as losing his twin. Almost. He still didn't understand how his brother's wife had turned everyone against him. Or why. He and Neasa had always been friends.

He stared into the dancing flames, taking comfort from their light and warmth. But even with the crackle of the fire, the night was too quiet. It was Beltane, and spring was here, in spite of all of Cathair's troubles. It was a night for raised voices and laughter.

So he sang to the fire. His heart was too heavy for a joyful tune, but he managed a thankful song.

A beautiful woman appeared in the firelight. She was clad only in long hair that shone like burnished gold in the flickering light. Her eyes were the color of the sea at dawn, and her skin pale as the foam that swirled on its surface.

Cathair's voice faltered. The woman frowned at the loss of the music, and vanished like mist in the sunlight.

Cathair stared at the empty air. She'd been a fairy, then,

or some other wild, unknowable creature. It was a night for magic, after all. Such creatures were dangerous. But she'd looked lonely.

Cathair knew loneliness.

He forced his voice into spirited reel. The fairy reappeared turning and spinning, stomping and clapping, all to the rhythm of his voice. He watched her go around the fire once, then twice. The sorrow lifted from his heart. On the third circle, he joined her.

Her laugh rang in his ears, harmonized with his voice. Her skin radiated heat like a banked fire. They danced till Cathair's breath grew ragged, till his songs were gasped fragments.

He'd forgotten what happiness felt like.

He held her hand in his. She didn't try to pull away. "I thank you for the dance, and for the music," she whispered. Her voice was like distant birdsong, carried by a summer wind. "What boon would you ask of me in return?"

"A name to call you," Cathair said.

She laughed. "Not my true name?"

"I have no desire to chain you."

"You have wisdom, as well as a beautiful voice and a handsome face. You may call me Aodhamair." She brushed her fingers along his cheek, leaving a trail of heat.

"Aodhamair," Cathair repeated. "A beautiful name. It suits you."

Aodhamair threw her head back and laughed. "You do please me. Come. Let us dance to a different song." She pulled him to the ground, warmed it beneath them with her burning skin and golden hair.

Eventually, the fire burned down, and the dawn crept across the sky, first gray, then with a full rainbow of colors. They watched the sunrise together.

She would have to leave soon. The thought cracked the

3

edges of Cathair's already-broken heart.

"I will grant you a boon," Aodhamair said. "Because you did not ask for one, and because you are worthy."

She pressed a delicately wrought silver ring into his hand. Cathair remembered Fial buying it last summer. "Your twin gave this to a village girl. She threw it into the forest after he was killed. She feared that his wife's jealousy would demand her head as well. Take this ring to your brother's lover, offer her your protection, and she will testify that it was not you who killed your beloved twin.

"Neasa killed Fial?"

Aodhamair nodded. "Your brother died at her hand. She was angry at his betrayal."

"Why accuse me?" Cathair asked.

Aodhamair shrugged. "Perhaps she thought you knew, that you helped him hide his affair."

"No. He never told me." Cathair would have tried to stop him.

He stared down at the ring. Proof. Proof that he was falsely accused. Proof that would allow him to win his life back. But what was there to go back to, now? His return would ruin Neasa. Fial was already gone. Everyone he'd trusted had turned against him.

"I—I would ask for another boon," Cathair said.

Aodhamair arched an eyebrow. "This does not please you?"

"Not as much as you do."

"Name your boon," she said. He thought he heard a quaver in her voice.

"I would stay with you."

"You do not understand what you ask."

Cathair shrugged. "Then tell me."

"I could become mortal and stay with you. But how can I

know that you will not betray me as your brother betrayed his wife?"

"I can't come with you? Become—what it is that you are?"

"It is possible. But you would lose all memory of your mortal life. Your twin would then be truly lost to you."

Fial had betrayed Neasa, lied to Cathair. To everyone. The memories weren't worth staying for. "He is already lost to me."

"Is your anger on his wife's behalf, or your own? Is it his infidelity or the fact that he didn't trust you with it that twists in your gut?" Aodhamair asked.

Cathair stroked her hand. "Neither was right."

Aodhamair stared up at the rising sun. Her face glowed. "I do not wish to stay here."

"Let me come with you," Cathair said. "My life is lost to me—even if I can regain my place, it's not mine anymore. Let me leave it behind and forget."

"That is truly your wish? There is no undoing this choice."

Cathair nodded. "My feet are ready for a new path."

"Very well," she said, standing, as glorious in the sunlight as in the firelight. She offered him her hand. "Come. It's time to go."

Cathair took her hand.

<div style="text-align:center">~~~</div>

May Flowers

May 2012

For Linda Vorp

My wonderful, supportive grandmother wanted me to write her a country story. With flowers. The story is almost as sweet as she is.

Gail threw together a picnic lunch—thick slices of ham on crusty bread, an apple, and a fresh slice of pound cake—and tied it up in a bandanna. She darted out into the spring sunshine and made her way to the brook. She had a pile of chores to do, not to mention spring cleaning, but no one minded if she took her lunch outside, as long as she got back on time.

She always got back on time.

Flowers bobbed in the cool breeze. Yellow daffodils and bright purple crocuses swayed next to bowing snowdrops, and pale pink tulips clustered together along the path. Petals from the apple blossoms drifted through the air like sweet-smelling snow.

Gail flopped down onto the new grass, peeled off her shoes, and dangled her feet into the frigid rushing water. She closed her eyes. Warm sunlight spread across her cheeks, and the brook's burble joined with the singing birds and buzzing bees in a lovely springtime symphony.

Soft footsteps approached. Anger spiked through Gail's belly. This was the only time she had to herself. Why was someone disturbing her? She waited for whoever it was to say something. Maybe they'd go away if she just ignored them. But curiosity tugged at her. She opened her eyes.

A bowling pin-sized man wrestled with her lunch, pulling at the knots ineffectually. The bundle was over half as big as he was.

Gail shook off her shock. "Hey! What do you think you're doing?"

The little man shot her an alarmed look, hefted her bandanna, and took off.

Gail chased him. Rocks bit into her bare feet, but the thief was staggering under the weight of his prize, and Gail caught him quickly. She pulled him off of her lunch, and held it in one hand and him in the other.

"Unhand me!" he shouted, "You nasty giant stupidface!"

Gail shook him—not hard enough to hurt him, just enough to quiet him down. "You were stealing my food," she said.

"I was not."

"You were too!"

"Prove it."

Gail held up her lunch. "I caught you with it."

"That's not yours. It's mine. I found it. You're the stealer. Give it back!"

Gail sighed. "I must be dreaming."

"Yeah! Dreaming that the tasty food is yours! Stealer!"

The little man was painfully thin. Gail could feel his tiny ribs. His heart beat as fast as a bird's, and he couldn't have weighed more than three pounds. Her lunch was heavier.

Gail set him down, then unwrapped her lunch before he could run. She ripped her sandwich in half, and handed the larger half to him. He snatched it and started nibbling the edges of the bread. "I suppose we can share," he said.

"What's your name?" Gail asked.

"Ruffo," he said.

"I'm Gail."

Ruffo continued gnawing on his half. He eyed the apple. "Split that too?"

Gail nodded. She split the skin along the apple's circumference with her fingernail, then twisted the fruit apart into two equal halves.

Ruffo finished his sandwich and his half of the apple. His frantic pace slowed somewhat. "Why're you here? Not with the other giants, in the giant house?"

Gail shrugged. "I like the flowers."

"Flowers are nice," Ruffo said. He was eyeing the cake, now.

Gail extended the whole piece.

Ruffo stared at it. Then he wrapped his arms around it and tore it in half. "We split," he said.

Gail smiled at him. "Okay."

They finished eating in silence. "Well, I need to get back." Gail pulled her shoes back on.

"You come back tomorrow?" Ruffo asked.

"I'll try," Gail said.

*

Storm clouds threatened the next day. The cook clucked at Gail as she wrapped up her lunch. "You're gonna get rained on."

Gail shrugged. "I won't melt."

She ran to the brook, and found the entire hillside covered with flowers. Tiny violets and forget-me-nots and others that she'd never seen before crowded around the path like a carpet. The air smelled like magic.

Ruffo walked out of the flowers, his tiny chest puffed up with pride. "For you," he said.

Gail blinked back tears. It was too much for half a sandwich and some cake. She untied and extended her lunch. "Here, as a thank you."

Ruffo took it and tore the sandwich in half. "We split," he said.

<p style="text-align:center">~~~</p>

A Diamond in the Sky

June 2012

For the Stefko Family

My mother-in-law told me to write whatever I wanted. So I wrote this. I love the full lyrics to "Twinkle, Twinlke, Little Star."

Delilah snaked her arm into the station's broken support thruster. If she could just get the stabilizer loose, she might be able to get it fixed. If not, they were going to have to order a new one from Earth.

No one wanted that.

She planted her magnetized boots and pulled. The stabilizer didn't budge. She sighed and punched it.

The thruster exploded. The force pushed her away from the station. Her safety line caught, held for an instant, then snapped.

The world went white.

*

Delilah's breath echoed in her helmet. The filtered air tasted thin and smelled like sweat. For a second, she had no idea where she was. Then memory rushed back.

She checked her air—she didn't have much left. Then she maneuvered herself around, looking for the station. She managed not to cry out when she saw it. It was so far away. She'd never get back in time.

She was dead already.

At least the station was still there. It looked like the explosion had been limited to the thruster. She hoped everyone else was okay.

She stared at the stars, wondered how long her body would drift.

Her suit dinged, and her O2 bar flashed. "I know," she whispered. Talking wasted oxygen, but that hardly mattered.

No one was coming for her.

Her radio crackled, and Tony's voice cut across the vacuum. "Delilah? Are you awake?"

"Yeah."

"I'm sorry."

Her stomach twisted. Of course they'd made Tony monitor her. Tony, who wrote bad poetry, remembered her birthday, sang like an angel, and had no idea that she was in love with him.

"We weren't sure you were alive," Tony said. "There was an explosion."

"I know."

"We—we can't get to you in time."

"I know."

She couldn't tell him now. It—it wasn't fair. But maybe she could have a dying wish. "Tony, would you—would you sing for me?"

"I don't know what to sing," he whispered.

"Anything," Delilah said. The silence stretched. Her chest started to ache. "Please."

"Twinkle, twinkle little star," Tony sang.

"How I wonder what you are.

Up above the world so high,

like a diamond in the sky.

When the blazing sun is gone,

When he nothing shines upon,

Then you show your little light,

Twinkle, twinkle, all the night.

Then the traveller in the dark,
Thanks you for your tiny spark,
He could not see which way to go,
If you did not twinkle so.

In the dark blue sky you keep,
And often through my curtains peep,
For you never shut your eye,
Till the sun is in the sky.

As your bright and tiny spark,
Lights the traveller in the dark.
Though I know not what you are,
Twinkle, twinkle, little star.

Twinkle, twinkle, little star.
How I wonder what you are.
Up above the world so high,
Like a diamond in the sky."

Delilah's breathing grew frantic. She closed her eyes and listened.

Tony's voice broke, but he kept singing. "Twinkle, twinkle, little star, how I wonder what you are. How I wonder what you are."

Then his voice was the only sound, and Delilah drifted away.

~~~
~~~

To the Dawn Star

July 2012

My aunt asked for a story about a hawk. They have a special meaning to her. This story is based on a Native American myth, though I did alter the ending pretty drastically.

Sosondowah stood by the entrance to the Goddess of Dawn's lodge and kept watch. He watched the stars wheel overhead. He watched the owls fly silently through the night air. He watched for foes that he knew would never come. The only thing he truly guarded was Dawn's vanity.

But she was as powerful as she was vain, and his punishment would be severe if he displeased her.

He watched as a woman crept out of her longhouse and slipped through the forest.

His attention sharpened.

The woman stopped in a clearing. She glanced around, making certain that she was alone. Then she started to sing in a voice so pure it reached the heavens.

She turned her face to the moonlight. Her voice held Sosondowah's heart, and her beauty pierced it. Then her song faltered. She looked around again. "Hello?" She glanced around again, then up at the sky, once. She rubbed her arms, as if chilled, then hurried back to her home.

*

Gendewitha and her sisters helped their mother plant corn. Spring birds flitted from tree to tree, singing their sweet songs. Gendewitha tried not to envy them as she trudged through the field.

At least the feeling of being watched had finally passed.

A bluebird landed on her arm, and she dropped her bag of corn. The bird stared at her, its black eyes uncommonly intense.

It sang a few notes, then flew away.

Gendewitha stared after it. How did it know her song? Who had been watching her last night?

*

Sosondowah stood at his post. He hoped that his turmoil didn't show on his face. Spring had stretched into summer, and he had only dared to slip away once. At least he had managed to overhear her name.

He watched Gendewitha whenever he could, but he longed to do more. He wanted to speak with her, to woo her, to marry her. If anyone had tried to invade Dawn's lodge while she was within view, he would never have noticed them.

Dawn was within now, asleep. She could wake at any moment. But she usually slept through the day.

Gendewitha was alone, fetching water for their crops.

He couldn't wait any longer. He transformed into a blackbird and flew to her.

*

A blackbird landed on Gendewitha's water pot and stared at her with the same intense eyes that the bluebird had. Shivers ran down her spine. "What are you?" she whispered.

In response, the blackbird sang her a song.

It was the song she sang to the moon, subtly altered, edged with longing and magic.

Then the bird flew away.

"Wait!" she reached out for its black wing, but it was gone.

She stood in the moonlight for a long time before she sang that night. But when she sang, she sang the bird's song.

*

Sosondowah could hear Dawn tossing and turning inside her lodge, but he couldn't wait any longer. Summer had deepened to autumn. Gendewitha still sang his song every night, but by day her father was entertaining suitors for her hand.

If he didn't act now, he might lose her forever. With one final glance back, he transformed into a hawk and flew down to her.

*

Gendewitha stood next to her father, looking modestly at the ground while men argued about her worth. She fought against resentment—against a feeling that something greater was being stolen from her.

Where was her bird? She could still sense him watching her while she sang—why didn't he come to her?

Then she heard wingbeats, and great talons wrapped around her arms and lifted her into the air.

She looked up at the giant hawk, and it looked back at her with intense black eyes.

Joy spiked through Gendewitha's heart, and she sang.

*

Sosondowah landed outside of Dawn's lodge and transformed into his true shape. "I am Sosondowah," he said.

Gendewitha's eyes widened—she recognized the name. "Why have you brought me here?" she asked.

"I would wed you, if you would have me," he said.

She looked him up and down, then nodded. "I would."

Dawn swept out of her lodge, her eyes dark with rage. "How dare you!" She slapped Sosondowah hard across the face, knocking him off of his feet. A great weight pinned him down.

She turned to Gendewitha. "You do not belong here, woman."

Gendewitha raised her chin. "Perhaps not. But I was invited."

Sosondowah struggled against Dawn's hold. He had to protect Gendewitha.

A slow smile spread across Dawn's face. "I suppose you were. But inviting you was not his place. It is mine."

She grabbed Gendewitha's arm. Pure white light spread from her hand, turning skin and flesh to shimmering fire. Gendewitha screamed as Dawn transformed her into a star. "It would be rude to turn you away," Dawn said.

Dawn threw Gendewitha high into the eastern sky. The new star flew away, growing smaller and smaller, until she was a twinkling point of light. For a moment, she hung high overhead. Then she fell. Sosondowah screamed her name, and she froze just above the horizon.

"She will herald my approach, be my Dawn Star." Dawn smirked at Sosondowah. "And you will forever be able to watch her without having her."

Dawn let him go and reentered her lodge.

Sosondowah stared at the door for a long moment, then at the bright star in the east. He imagined watching her for the rest of time. He wondered if she could see him, if stars could yearn for their lover or cry from loneliness.

He wondered if she could still sing.

He transformed into his hawk shape. He made his wings wide, for his journey would be long. He darkened his feathers, to hide better from Dawn, and grew his downy layer thick, for the space between stars was colder than any winter.

He left Dawn's door unguarded, and flew into the sky.

~~~
~~~

Out in the Rain

July 2012

For Paul Stefko

My husband wanted to challenge me, so he asked for cyberpunk noir set after a job gone bad. I don't think this is exactly what he had in mind, but he seemed to like it anyway.

Talia picked her way through the shattered revolving door. Singed bills fluttered in the pre-storm breeze as she ducked beneath police tape and took in the scene.

The bomb had taken out the vault door and blown half the back wall away.

It was impressive work.

She weaved between uniforms until she spotted Detective Summers kneeling next to one of the still-smoking bodies.

Summers looked up from the corpse and their eyes met.

Talia could read Summers' slightest reactions—one of her implants translated microexpressions. Surprise, followed by hurt, then relief flashed across Summers face.

The relief was a surprise.

Things must be bad.

Summers stood and walked over. "What are you doing here?"

No smile, no secret welcome wink. And her voice sent a spike of longing through her heart. Talia was glad that Summers didn't go for implants. She crossed her arms. "I heard the explosion. Thought maybe I could help."

Summers shrugged. "Bank job gone bad. Not your normal gig."

Talia's normal gig was cheating spouses. But she'd helped out on dozens of cases. Before.

Summers' cell phone buzzed, and she pulled it out of her pocket. "I should take this."

Talia's phone was wired into her skull. So was her signal interceptor.

She hesitated for a second, then hacked into Summers' feed. It was simple. She'd told Summers to update her hardware a million times.

"But we've had these tickets for weeks!"

An unfamiliar female voice. Unwelcome jealousy curled in Talia's belly.

"I warned you about making plans." Summers was using her placating tone. Soft. Loving. Wrenchingly familiar.

She'd moved on.

Which, Talia reminded herself, was what she wanted. She tuned the call out, downloaded the surveillance video, and turned back to the crime scene. She scanned for things that unaugmented eyes might miss. She scanned the blast pattern, the floating bills, the mop abandoned in a spreading pool of tepid water.

The pieces fell into place.

After a few minutes, Summers wandered back over. "See anything?"

Talia shrugged. "Seems simple enough."

"My boys think they were set to blow the safe, got suspicious of each other, started shooting, and lost track of time."

Talia arched an eyebrow. "Do you buy that?"

"No. And neither do you. No one just forgets about a bomb. And the surveillance feeds cut out too conveniently."

A year ago, Summers would have needed Talia to tell her that.

"What's your theory, then?" Talia asked.

Summers shrugged. "Don't have one yet."

"You'll get there," Talia said. She walked out of the bank.

Summers didn't call her back.

It started to rain.

*

She stood on a bridge, her face bare to the thunderstorm. The swollen, gray river rolled on under her feet.

She didn't know why she'd gone to the bank in the first place. She'd called things off. She didn't want to be tied down. Didn't want to be needed.

She didn't know what she wanted.

Summers approached, wrapped in a sensible coat and clutching a bright red umbrella.

She stood shoulder to shoulder with Talia. Rain drummed on the umbrella.

Talia missed the rain on her face, but the feel of Summers shoulder against hers was worth it.

"Tell me what happened," Summers said.

"You'll figure it out. Maybe you have already."

Summers' shoulder shifted in a shrug. "Maybe. Tell me anyway."

"Your corpses didn't know about the bomb. Someone else planted it. It was in the wall. Buried deep. Whoever planted that bomb—that's who cut the vid feeds, tricked the robbers into turning on each other, and took your missing money."

"How did you know about the money?"

It was Talia's turn to shrug. "You're looking for the janitor. Used to work nights, got promoted to dayshift. Got the money out in a bucket."

They stood together for a while, listening to the rain.

"It's not serious," Summers said.

"I don't know what you're talking about."

Summers laughed. "Why do you think I keep that old phone?"

"You knew I'd listen."

"I hoped."

Talia's heart ached. "You're better off without me."

"Maybe."

Rain fell. Cars hissed by.

"Maybe someday I'll get tired of waiting for you." Summers pulled a second umbrella out of her pocked and pressed the first into Talia's hand. "Or maybe someday you'll have enough sense to come in out of the rain."

Summers walked away.

Talia stayed and watched the river rolling by.

~~~
~~~

Everyone's a Winner

August 2012

For Daksha and Eesha

Balendra Sutharshan didn't give me a prompt, but he asked that I dedicate the story to his daughters. A friend suggested a country fair theme, since it went up on my website in the heart of fair season. And I've always loved the Duck Game.

Maya clutched her father's hand as they wandered through the fair. New sights, sounds, and smells bombarded her. The scents of fried dough, powdered sugar, hot sausage, and cotton candy warred with manure, sweat, and machine oil. All around, people barked about games, shrieked on rides, and greeted one another in booming voices. The carnival rides creaked and groaned. When she could see past the sea of legs around her, she caught glimpses of bright plastic jewelry, discarded food, painted trailers, and stuffed animals.

Her father's hand was the only thing that seemed real.

Then, she saw the ducks.

Tiny plastic ducks bobbed around a watery track. A pale young woman with too-black hair and crooked teeth beckoned Maya over. "Come play the Duck Game!" she called. "Everyone's a winner!"

Maya tugged on her father's hands. "I want to play with the ducks!" she said.

He smiled down at her and let her drag him over. He peeled limp dollar bills out of his wallet and passed them to the Duck Girl.

Maya stared at the ducks as they floated by. They came in more colors than she'd expected—yellow, red, blue, green, and purple ducks competed for her attention.

It was important to pick the right one.

Finally, her hand darted forward, and she snatched a green duck. She held it between her hands and kissed its bright orange bill.

"Maya," her father said, his voice full of warning.

Maya ignored him. The hard plastic softened under her fingers, transforming to downy green feathers. Its tiny feet kicked, and its tiny heart fluttered.

The Duck Girl held out a small stuffed animal. "Here's your prize!" she said.

Maya ignored her. She had to focus on her duck, or something might go wrong.

"Stop it, Maya," her father said.

Maya's duck quacked, and Maya laughed. The Duck Girl stared. She reached out and touched the green duckling's bill. It snapped at her.

"Be nice, Ducky," Maya whispered.

Maya's father gripped her shoulder. He was ready to run if the Duck Girl started screaming.

Maya didn't think she would.

The Duck Girl stared at the duck for another long moment. Maya's father stood very still.

Then, the Duck Girl pulled another stuffed animal—a pink unicorn—from the shelf behind her. "Can you—can you do that again?" she asked.

Maya's father frowned at both of them. Maya gave him her best pleading expression. The Duck Girl's eyes darted between them. "Please?" she said.

Maya's father sighed. "Don't tell anyone where you got it."

The Duck Girl squealed in delight. Maya's father took her duckling from her, gently, and let Maya take the unicorn.

Changing it was easier—it wasn't made of plastic.

When she was done, the Duck Girl handed her the first

stuffed animal. It was a tiny bear wearing a black bow tie. "This is yours," she said, her voice soft. "Everyone's a winner."

Maya's father picked her up. "We should go," he said.

Maya waved at the Duck Girl.

The Duck Girl held her tiny unicorn close to her chest, and waved back.

~~~
~~~

Top of the Game

September 2012

For Dylan, Kiefer, and Lleyton

Michael Slaysman wanted a story based on ice hockey with elements from the Mayan ballgame. I decided that it should happen in space. This is the very first story I completed for this project, and I was very happy with the ending.

I spun in a fast, uncontrolled circle, my mouth guard half-out, my visor cracked, and my own blood floating in front of me in a spray of perfectly round orbs.

Gloved hands pulled the heavy, black rubber ball out of my grip, and the other player pushed off of me, turning my spin into a plummet, straight toward the curved ice wall.

I blinked away the haze and disorientation that follows any good hit, and the roar of the crowd—piped in from stadiums across the galaxy where fans watched us on screens taller than houses—hit my ears like a hammer.

They were chanting my name.

I kicked hard, reigniting the rockets on my skates. It would be too late to avoid colliding with the wall, but maybe I could keep from breaking my legs.

I hit with a crunch, and impact screamed up my bones. My skates shrieked across the ice. I pushed off, aimed directly back toward the action. My knees would punish me later, but the crowd loved it.

My uniform had sealed over the worst of the slash across my shoulder, but my forehead was still leaking blood in a trail of red blobs. The crowd loved that, too.

I was moving fast—faster than was safe, faster than most players could manage. I stripped the ball from the desperately thin, clumsy-handed rookie who'd stolen it from me, turned in midflight—a move no fresh-from-planetside twerp would dare—and raced back toward the other team's goalie.

Amanda Burgess glared up at me. She was one of the only players who'd been up here longer than me. She was good. A grin stretched across my face. I'd left the rest of both of our teams behind. It was between her and me.

She grinned back. Like a wolf. Or a shark. I feinted left, moved right, kicked my left leg to flare its rocket to full power, and spun around her. Pain flared in my injured shoulder. Amanda slammed into me, but it was too late. The ball was away, flying straight toward the hoop that she'd been guarding.

She swore, and I whooped in triumph as the ball sailed straight through. The lights flashed, then went out. The crowd was cut off in mid-roar. We floated in perfect darkness, perfect silence. Till Amanda muttered, "Nice shot, Perez. But you know, that kid's probably gonna starve, now."

*

The team nurse scowled as she sewed me up. "Two inches to the right, and you'd have bled out in there."

I shrugged, and she growled at me to keep still. Two inches wasn't the closest it'd ever been.

I tried not to see the rookie's face behind my eyelids. Where did Amanda get off, spouting crap like that?

The nurse washed and bandaged my forehead.

And where did I get off, feeling sympathy for the kid? He'd almost killed me out there.

I'd come up here over a decade ago, an undercover reporter looking for an exposé about the dangers of extreme space-based sport. And I'd fallen in love with it. Sure, things were crooked. If you didn't win, didn't get the fans' notice, you had a hard time getting access to medical aid, decent equipment, and food.

But I almost always won, even in the beginning. I'd never been as hungry as the kid looked.

The perks of being a star are nice. Private room in the spinning section, private shower that never runs out of hot water. Millions of adoring fans, plenty of them women willing to pay to hook up with me on virtual. One even came to visit once, for the "full zero-G experience."

But that's not why I stayed, why I dropped contact with my editor and my family.

I stayed for the game.

I'd never felt alive, living the life I left behind. That life had been about striving—always reaching for the dreams that stayed just out of reach. Here, on the station—and in the game— I do what I want. Take the things I want. And I keep them. Because I can.

"Sooner or later, this game is going to kill you," the nurse said. "You know that, right?"

I nodded. Of course I knew. It killed all of us, eventually.

But it was better than retiring.

*

I sent the losing team food. Dehydrated shit, nothing great. I could have afforded better. But doing it made me feel good.

Amanda came to my door the next day. She looked strange without her uniform and pads. I wondered if she had as many scars as I did.

"That was unexpected," she said.

I shrugged. "They'll still die if they can't make it on their own."

She shrugged. "Still, it was good of you. A kindness. I wanted to say thanks. Most of them are sweet kids."

"Why not thank me by doing it yourself next time? I'm sure you can afford it."

She laughed. "I can afford better. And you could have, too."

I shrugged. "Don't want to spoil them."

She nodded, slowly. "Maybe I will. Maybe it'll be your team, next time."

"Want to come in?" I asked. "Have a drink or two?"

She looked startled for a second, then her shark grin spread across her face. "Sure. Why not?"

I led her inside. Maybe we'd end up comparing scars.

It was nice to win without anyone else losing.

~~~
~~~

Feeding the Master

October 2012

I owed my lovely friend Alexis Covato for a painting she did for me, and she agreed to trade part of my debt for a story. I wrote it for Halloween, so I was going for creepy.

Stanley initiated a standard scan and watched the numbers scroll across his screen. "That's not right," he muttered. He stopped the test and restarted it. He stared at the image on the screen. His mind drifted. He reached forward, and jumped when his fingers hit smooth plastic.

He shook himself.

"Captain, I'm getting abnormal readings," Stanley said. "These are not indicative of a black hole at all."

The captain glanced over. "What are they indicative of?"

Stanley tapped his screen and scowled. "I have no idea, ma'am."

"Let's send a probe."

*

The probe passed what appeared to be an event horizon and continued toward the anomaly. The readings cut off just before it made contact. Its readings matched Stanley's, but didn't offer any additional insight.

"This is all very unusual," the first officer muttered. "We've never seen—"

The ship lurched forward violently.

"Diane! What are you doing?" the first officer shouted at the pilot.

The pilot shook herself, then yelped and pulled her hand off of the accelerator. "I don't know what happened," she said. "My hand must have slipped."

"It was a poorly timed slip," the captain said, her voice grim. "We've passed the event horizon."

*

The shift changed, and Stanley went to his quarters while the senior staff wrestled with saving their lives.

He felt odd. A strange anticipation danced in his belly. He remembered his strange spell earlier, and wondered if the pilot, Diane, had felt something similar.

He went to bed and dreamed of white creatures that skittered on their bellies, and of a dark, all-seeing lord.

It was an oddly pleasant dream.

*

The ship continued to fall toward the anomaly. Stanley fought against excitement swirling in his belly. He shouldn't be excited. He should be terrified.

But the excitement wouldn't go away. He felt giddy—couldn't concentrate. He fought to keep his hands away from his instruments—he didn't trust them anymore.

He noticed that Diane was actually sitting on her hands.

The head engineer finished tapping something into the computer. "Okay, captain, the engines are ready. This should work."

"Let's get out of here," the captain said.

The engineer pushed a final button.

Nothing happened.

Stanly and Diane were both touching their screens.

The rest of the bridge crew stared at them. Both stepped back. Diane started crying. "I don't know what happened!"

Stanly didn't remember moving his hands. He had no idea what he'd done. "I—I think we should be locked up," he said.

The first officer nodded to the security officers. "I agree."

*

Stanley buried his face in his hands. Diane was still crying. He searched his mind for what he'd done, but his memory was blank.

He should be feeling shame. He should be horrified that something had gotten into his body and moved him like a puppet. He should be afraid for his life.

Instead, all he felt was that same, mounting excitement.

He wondered if Diane's tears were real.

*

As they fell, gravity grew. Whatever the anomaly was, it had incredible mass, and moving became more and more difficult. Stanley was pinned to his cot in the brig, like a bug on a corkboard. He wondered how long until he was crushed.

He still wasn't afraid.

They hit the anomaly with a dull thunk that reverberated through the whole ship. The lights sputtered and died. Dim emergency lights pulsed, giving eerie, displaced flashes of vision.

Stanley understood how he needed to move. Rolling was hard, but then he landed on the floor. His wrists and ankles were wrong when he looked at them, so he turned his eyes away. The lights pulsed, and he saw that Diane was on the floor, too. Her hands and feet were all flat on the floor.

"There's something wrong with us," she said. But there was joy in her voice.

Stanley skittered forward. The energy field that held them in their cells had failed. Life support would soon follow. His elbows and knees burned at first, then the sensation faded. "Our master is waiting," he said. He didn't know where the words came from, but they were true.

Diane grinned. "Our master," she repeated, savoring the words. "Yes."

The lifts weren't working, but they wrenched the doors open and scrambled up the elevator shaft. They slipped into the bridge.

The lights pulsed, and he saw that the others were pinned to their seats, or on the floor where they'd fallen. The captain tried to lift her head. "What are you doing?" she asked. Her voice was weak—the gravity would soon be too much for her lungs.

"We must feed," Diane said.

Revulsion spiked through Stanley's gut, followed by glee. She was right. They needed to feed, so that their master could feed. So that he could escape the prison he'd been locked in for so long.

Diane skittered over to the first officer. He managed to cry out as she sank her teeth into his leg. But he could not thrash, could not fight her.

Stanley went to the captain. The terror in her eyes didn't please Stanley. But his master hungered.

He started at the captain's throat. There was no reason not to make it quick—she'd always been a strong leader, and a kind woman.

Her blood was hot on Stanley's tongue. It slid down his throat like water.

His master needed more.

But there were enough people on board. They would feast, and then their master would gather them to himself and fly through the stars, looking for new prey.

Diane cackled with joy, and Stanley joined in.

~~~
~~~

We Wait, and We Hope

November 2012

Pete Butler wanted a "cheerful apocalypse" story. I'm pretty happy with how this turned out. It's more experimental than most of my other work, but I had fun writing it.

The adults all succumb to the sleep at the same time. Our parents slump, boneless, to the floor. Teachers sag onto their desks, cashiers fall next to their registers, bike couriers tumble sideways and roll. The smallest children sleep as well. Babies curl on their mothers' breasts, soft and warm and quiet.

We shake them. We scream. We cry. They do not wake, do not stir. Their injuries heal quickly.

We pour careful sips of water down still throats, but they do not seem to need it. We cannot feed them, but they do not grow thin. Their chests rise and fall. We drag them to hospitals, roll them to prevent bedsores that never threaten to form.

We do not know what else to do.

We turn to the internet.

The sleep is global, as far as we can tell. We begin to worry about the others—the ones without canned food lined on shelf after shelf. We find pilots among our oldest, with fresh licenses and butterfly-filled stomachs. We fly planes around the world to share cell phones that we dig from adult pockets.

Our numbers swell.

One of us blames a rival nation—he claims their adults are faking sleep. He threatens violence. Then his voice falls silent. The sleep takes him. Some of us feel fear, others hope and relief.

We put him in a hospital bed with the others.

We distribute food as evenly as we can. Our systems grow streamlined, efficient. Our supplies do not dwindle. It is suspiciously easy.

We debate on what is happening. Our phones never lose power, the internet never falters. We no longer get sick. Our adults do not wake.

We wonder who is really asleep—are we the ones dreaming?

Some of us become farmers, and dirt darkens our fingernails. Others are pilots, boat captains, teachers, artists. We all vote when choices must be made. We all communicate with each other. Our voices are all equal. We are proud of ourselves.

Some of us hope this is some kind of test—that we will pass it eventually. Some blame aliens, others God. Others are thankful and try to live in the series of peaceful moments, without too much worry for the future.

We feed ourselves. We live our lives.

Time passes. The sleeping do not age. We fall in love. We start families. A few of us look older than our mothers.

Some of us still cry for them. Some of us don't.

We wait, and work to understand.

We wait, and watch for signs of waking.

We wait, and we hope.

~~~
~~~

Finding Christmas

December 2012

For Savannah

Savannah Klunder asked me to write her a creepy story. Since I'd be posting it in December, I went with a Christmas theme. I worried that it might not be dark enough, but she assured me she didn't want it to be too sad.

Angry, frozen snowflakes hissed against Derrick's window. Cold seeped through cracks in his Dad's stupid, sagging house and gathered around his ankles.

He pulled his afghan off the bed and pulled it to his chin. The scratchy yarn smelled like gingerbread and sage incense. Like Mom. Like home.

It masked the sawdust-and-paint smell of Dad's house and helped him to forget that this was the worst Christmas ever.

At least Santa should be able to find him here. That's why Mom had left him when she went away with Uncle Marty. She called every night, and Derrick tried to pretend he was happy. He tried not to feel a spiteful spike of happiness at the guilt in her voice. He tried to forget that none of his friends believed in Santa.

A dull red glow grew in the swirling snow.

"Rudolph!" Derrick whispered, his doubts forgotten. The light grew closer, brighter. He could almost see reindeer shapes. Was that shadow the sleigh?

The wind screamed, pushing the glow away, buffeting it down. The scream stretched, and the glow faltered, then flickered.

Then died.

Derrick cried out, but his voice was lost beneath the wind's cruel laugh. He gathered his afghan around his shoulders, ran down the unfinished stairs, shoved his feet into his boots, and ran out into the storm.

He saw a glimmer of red, and pushed toward it.

Snow pelted his face, clung to his eyelashes, and weighted down his boots. The wind pushed him back and howled. It was a rough, animal sound, but Derrick heard words in it. "Unwanted. Unloved. Burden."

He pushed toward the glow.

He heard a wet coughing, then he found them.

The red light from Rudolph's nose cast hellish shadows over the crumpled reindeer bodies. The sleigh was already half buried, and presents lay scattered about, their glittering paper torn and wet, their ribbons crooked, their corners crushed.

Santa slumped in the sleigh. His blood was black in the red light, and it stained his beard and the white fur trim of his suit. Derrick rushed to his side and shook him. His skin was cold. "Santa, wake up!"

Santa's eyes opened, focused. "Hello, Derrick," he said, his voice ragged and thick. "You should get back inside."

"I want to help."

Santa shook his head. "The cost is too great."

Tears burned down Derrick's cheeks. He could never help. He remembered holding his parents hands, trying to pull them back together.

The wind laughed.

"Please," Derrick said. "Let me help. I can do it."

The wind cackled and swirled around him, covering him in stinging snow. Ice crackled across his eyes, and he saw his mother.

She laughed and ran into the bright blue ocean. Uncle Marty followed, and they kissed.

Derrick wanted to look away, but he couldn't.

"I wish we could stay here forever," his mother said.

"We could, you know," Uncle Marty said. "I can work from anywhere."

Derrick's mother shook her head. "I can't."

"Why not?"

"You know why."

Uncle Marty kissed her again. "The kid would be fine without you. Why not live for yourself for a while?"

His mother shook her head. Derrick waited for her to get mad, to tell him that she'd never leave her son—that she didn't want to leave him, that he wasn't a burden. "I never even wanted kids," she whispered.

The ice on Derrick's eyes shattered, and he fell to his knees. The wind whispered one last word in his ear, then faded. The sky cleared.

Santa stood before him, his face sad and his beard whiter than the glistening snow. "Thank you, Derrick." He handed Derrick a present. "I hope this helps."

Then he was gone, and Derrick was alone with his tiny present. Penguins danced on the wrapping paper. He wanted to throw it into a snowbank.

He wiped his aching eyes and opened it.

Another vision appeared before him. His father, holding him as a baby, cooing. Then his father standing in a store dithering between two small bikes. The blue one had been Derrick's favorite birthday present ever.

His father, sitting in his new house alone, holding Derrick's old baseball glove and crying.

Then his mother, on the beach. "But I can't imagine my life without him, now. I couldn't leave him."

"Derrick!"

The vision faded as Derrick's father ran through the snow. He still smelled like sawdust and paint. "What the hell are you doing out here?"

"I was looking for Christmas," Derrick said. He took his father's warm hand between his.

His dad stared at Derrick for a long moment, then picked him up, even though he was really too big to carry anymore. "Did you find it?"

He smiled up at his Dad and breathed in the scent of home. "I think so."

~~~
~~~

Two by Sea

January 2013

For Rona

Katie Board wanted a story about a zombie shark. So, I wrote her one. This was one of the most difficult stories in the whole book for me. The core inspiration was so over-the-top that I had a hard time coming up with a story to match it. In the end, though, I think it worked out.

Trina scraped the last can of beans into a pot and lit the sailboat's tiny antique stove. Alan came down the steps and shook his head. "No fish. Again." He sighed. "There should be fish."

He hung his fishing pole on its hook, under one of the harpoons that the ship's former owner had collected.

Trina stirred the beans. "We have to land for supplies."

"Starving might be better," Alan said.

"We can't just give up. What if we're the last ones? Maybe we'll get lucky. Maybe the zombies have moved on. Or eaten each other."

Alan sighed and pushed both hands through his hair. "You're right. I'm sorry."

Trina handed him a spoon, and they ate their beans in silence.

"I'll go get us turned around," Alan said.

*

Dinner was a can of peas and a chocolate bar that Trina had been saving for a special occasion. They sat on the deck, watching the sunset. It was a beautiful evening.

She ate her chocolate slowly, despite the empty ache in her belly.

"One of us has to stay with the boat," she said.

Alan shook his head. "Hell no. We're not splitting up. We only have one gun."

"You'll sail back out once I'm off, then come back for me when I've got the supplies."

"No. We stick together."

Trina knew he was thinking about his girlfriend—they'd been separated in the first wave, and he'd never seen her again.

Trina had watched her family torn apart. She'd seen her son's broken body stand back up. She thought Alan had it better.

"We have to be smart about this," she said.

"You need someone to watch your back."

"I need a guaranteed escape route."

"Fine. But you're going to stay on the boat. I'll go for supplies," Alan said.

"You're the better sailor." She'd never even been on a sailboat, before the zombies came.

Alan frowned and turned away. "I'm going to fish." He grabbed his pole and thumped over to the starboard bow.

Something slammed against the front of the boat, and the deck rocked beneath their feet. Alan stumbled, started to fall. Trina screamed his name.

A huge shark exploded out of the calm water. It lunged at the edge of the boat, and its huge mouth chewed at the wooden railing. Huge chunks of flesh were missing along its cheeks, exposing jagged rows of teeth that glistened red in the fading light. Its black eyes were dull, and oozing bite marks marred its silvery flank.

Alan threw himself back, away from the shark, and scrambled back to Trina's side. The shark splashed back into the water, then lunged out again. The railing splintered, but held.

Trina ran into the cabin, grabbed the gun, and sprinted back up the stairs.

The shark fell back into the water, and Trina waited for it to try again.

Instead, the deck shuddered under her feet. Wood creaked and groaned. "Can it break through the hull?" she asked.

"I don't know. I have no idea how much of this the ship can take," Alan said. "We need to outrun it. I hope we're faster than it, at least over distance. I'll adjust the sails."

Trina thought of him scrambling around on the deck, his eyes on the sails, exposed. She imagined him losing his footing, falling straight into the shark's waiting jaws. "Wait. I can do it."

He shook his head. "I'm the better sailor."

*

The pounding stopped as they picked up speed.

They sailed all night. They stayed as far away from the railings as possible, and neither of them slept. Trina kept the gun on her person. Alan grabbed a harpoon and strapped a second one to his back.

They caught sight of land as the sun rose behind them.

Trina looked back as Alan slowed the boat and scanned the shore. A flicker of motion caught her eye, and she watched in horror as a fin emerged from the water. "Alan! It followed us!" she shouted. She pulled the gun to her shoulder.

The shark swam toward them. Trina could see its huge, battered body through the clear water, then it was flying through the air, straight at Alan.

She didn't know where its brain was.

Alan spun, his harpoon braced in front of him.

The shark landed on the point with a wet thunk. Alan went sprawling, but he managed to keep the harpoon between his flesh and the shark's snapping jaws.

Trina aimed at one of its eyes.

Its tail slammed into her stomach, and she dropped the gun. A bullet bit uselessly into the shark's flank. It rolled from

the impact, and the deck tilted. Trina grabbed the splintered
railing to keep from falling into the shark, and the gun slid under
its writhing body.

"Shoot it!" Alan screamed.

She couldn't get to the gun. But she could get to Alan.
She ducked under the thrashing tail and pulled the extra harpoon
off of Alan's back.

The shark smelled like seawater and decay.

She thrust the harpoon into its dead black eye with all of
her strength.

It went limp.

Alan pulled himself from under it. He examined
himself—he was covered in dark, angry bruises and bleeding
from a dozen scratches, but there were no bite marks. "You—
you saved us. Thank you." He ran his hands over his legs. "Are
you okay?"

Trina nodded. Her stomach hurt, but it was bearable.
"How are you?"

Alan pulled himself to his feet. "Surprised and relieved, I
guess. Tired. Hungry. I guess we'd better put in so you can get
the supplies."

Trina nodded. "You're okay with me going, now?"

He shrugged. "You killed a zombie shark with a harpoon.
If that's not a sign that you can take care of yourself, I don't know
what is."

Trina helped sail to shore. "I'll be back. I promise."

Alan kissed her cheek. "Be careful." He handed her a
harpoon.

She watched him sail out toward the rising sun, then
turned inland. She had work to do.

~~~
~~~

A Prom Princess of Mars

February 2013

For Deborah Lackey

My mother wanted another Martian Adventures story. This is set about five years after the other stories, which you can find at the end of this book. The Martian community has grown a lot since Jim and Ronnie first met.

Ronnie took a deep breath. She reminded herself that she shouldn't be nervous. That Jim was her best friend. And that if she waited, stupid Kristen might ask him first and ruin everything. "So, prom."

Jim nodded. "The very first on Mars."

"Want to go with me?" Ronnie asked.

Jim laughed. "Isn't the guy supposed to ask the girl?"

"Maybe on Earth. This is Mars."

"True."

"Well, do you want to go with me or not?"

"Of course I do."

Ronnie grinned. Take that, Kristen.

*

Jim's mother pulled a box out from under their couch. "Your grandmother sent this from Earth. I gave her your measurements, so it should fit."

Jim pulled the box open and stared down at the fine black material. "What is it?"

"A tuxedo. For you to wear to prom."

"Mom, nobody else is going to be wearing a tuxedo."

"Then you'll look better than everyone else. A black tux never goes out of style. Go on, try it on."

Jim sighed, but figured it'd be best to humor her. He pulled on the black pants, buttoned up the white shirt and red vest, and pulled the jacket on. Everything fit. He checked his reflection.

"Huh." He looked pretty good.

He wondered what Ronnie would think.

*

Ronnie burst into her family's quarters. "Mom!" she shouted.

Her mother poked her head out of the kitchen. "What's wrong, sweetie?"

"Jim's grandma sent him a tux."

"That was sweet of her."

"No it wasn't! It was terrible! Now what am I going to wear?"

She'd been planning on wearing her best dress—the one she wore to greet new people when they arrived on Mars. But Jim had seen her in that dozens of times. She needed something new. Something special.

It was their very first real date, after all.

Her mother tapped her lips. "I see your point."

Ronnie threw herself onto the couch. "This sucks."

"I have an idea." Her mom disappeared into her bedroom and came out few minutes later with a large storage box. "I can make you a new dress. I used to sew my own dresses all of the time."

Hope stirred in Ronnie's chest. "Where will we get the fabric?"

Her mom pulled out a red satin dress trimmed with black ribbon out of the box. "I'll start with this."

Ronnie's hope faded. The dress was tiny. "I wore that when I was five."

"Yes, but the material is still good. I can reuse it."

"I can't wear a mini dress to prom. Dad would flip."

"Go see if anyone else has any old clothes that they wouldn't mind us repurposing."

"Yes, Mom."

*

Two hours and half the station later, Ronnie came back home loaded down with old clothes. She dumped them on the kitchen table. "Will any of this work?"

Her mom combed through the pile. She pulled out one deep red blouse and a black lace skirt. "These might."

Her mother sewed, and she refused to let Ronnie look at her handiwork.

"I want it to be a surprise," she said, closing the door in her face.

"I'd rather have some input!" Ronnie shouted through the door.

"You're just going to have to trust me!"

*

Jim shifted his corsage from one hand to the other, wiped his palms on his tuxedo pants, and knocked on Ronnie's door. Her dad answered. "Hey, Jim. Come on in. She's almost ready." He crossed his arms over his chest. "She's very... excited about this whole thing." He sighed. "We're very fond of you Jim, and I trust that you won't—disappoint her."

Jim gulped. "I—I wouldn't dream of it, sir."

"Where are my shoes?" Ronnie ran down the stairs. Her hair was pinned up on top of her head and her eyes looked different. Bigger, somehow. And she looked incredible in her dress. It was long, and red, with black lace accents and a black ribbon belt.

"Oh, Jim! You're here!" Ronnie froze on the stairs and blushed. "I didn't realize. Well, what do you think?" She twirled for him. Her long skirt flowed around her ankles, and the back of the dress swooped down to just above her hips.

Jim stared. "You look amazing. Like a princess."

Ronnie's mother came down the stairs. "Oh, look, you even match."

Ronnie grinned at him. "It was meant to be."

Jim held out the box of flowers. "My mom got us roses."

"They're beautiful."

"Here, you wear this one on your wrist, and this one pins to me... somewhere."

"Let me help you with that," Ronnie's mom said.

"No, I can do it." Ronnie stepped close to him. She smelled different—like perfume and hairspray. Her breath was warm on his cheek. He wondered if she could feel his heart beating through his jacket.

Ronnie's mom turned to her dad. "What do you think of the dress?"

"Why doesn't it have a back?"

"Fabric shortage."

"Hmph."

Ronnie finished pinning the rose to Jim's lapel. "Come on. Let's go."

*

Jim and Ronnie swayed together in the decorated cafeteria. "Are you having fun?" he asked.

Ronnie nodded. Jim looked so handsome, and she loved dancing. And she had to admit, her mom had done a great job on the dress.

Someone tapped on Ronnie's shoulder, and she looked back. Kristen smiled at her. "Can I cut in?"

Ronnie's stomach dropped. Jim was so polite, and Kristen was his friend. He'd have to dance with her.

But his arms tightened around her. "Sorry, Kristen. We're in the middle of something. Maybe later?"

Kristen blinked, and for a second, guilt warred with the joy in Ronnie's belly. But Kristen just nodded. "Okay. Maybe later."

Jim twined his fingers through Ronnie's. She liked his hands. She liked everything about him.

"What were we in the middle of?" she asked.

"This."

He kissed her. His lips were warm, and tasted like fruit punch.

"Oh," Ronnie said, after he pulled away.

"I couldn't let you do that first, too, even if we are on Mars," he said.

Ronnie laid her head on his chest and listened to his heartbeat, and they danced.

~~~
~~~

Cuttlefish Skin

March 2013

Sabrina Zitzelberger asked for a story about cuttlefish. My favorite part of researching for this story was watching videos of them changing their skin.

Prana floated above the silty ocean bottom, shifting her skin color to match its color and visual texture. She spotted a shrimp scuttling along, but she didn't have time to stop for a snack. Her Teacher had sent for her.

She squeezed through the narrow opening to his cave and looked around. She couldn't see him. But then, she never could. She'd only glimpsed him once, as a flash of movement out of the corner of one eye.

His voice seemed to come from all around. "Good morning, Prana."

"Good morning, Teacher."

"You have proven yourself a worthy student, and I feel that it is time for me to give you your final test."

Fear flashed through her, and Prana fought to control her skin. "I don't know if I'm ready."

"You are."

Prana shrunk around her cuttle bone and sank toward the floor of the cave. "I'm listening."

"Your final test is to survive a full sun cycle in open water."

Prana's first impulse was to squirt ink at him. Or at least in whatever general direction she guessed he was in. "How will getting eaten help me master my skin?"

"It won't. Staying alive will."

"I'm afraid."

"That is wise. You came to me, Prana. If you wish to take what you've learned and leave, you are free to do so."

Prana remembered that fleeting glimpse of him. She had seen his striped limbs—that was how she was certain he was male. "What if I pass the test?" she asked.

"Then we will be equals."

"Would you mate with me?" Prana asked. Her Teacher was the only male she'd ever encountered who hadn't offered her his spermatophore, and she would gladly accept them.

"I would," he said.

She wanted to give her eggs the best chance she could. "I will try."

*

Prana floated toward the open water. Her skin rippled blue and green. She imagined herself growing transparent. She imagined a shark crushing her soft body in its jaws, grinding her cuttlebone to powdery fragments.

Schools of fish swam by, and she matched their silver flanks. The sun cycle crawled by. She focused on tiny variations in the light, and matched them with her skin. The subtle work was draining.

A shark swam by.

It didn't even slow down, and she bobbed in its wake.

The light of the sun cycle finally faded, replaced by the silvery glow of the moon. She matched the patterns in the dark water effortlessly.

She floated back to her Teacher's cave. She squeezed inside, and showed him what she'd learned.

His striped arms appeared in front of her, and she reached for him.

<p style="text-align:center">~~~</p>

A Happy Valentine's Day

Bonus Story

For Amy Treadwell

*I wrote this story on Valentine's Day for my Kickstarter backers. It's
a sweet, happy story with light fantasy elements.*

Kimmy clutched the scissors so tight that her hand ached,
and her damp palms left dark smudges on the red construction
paper. She sat in the center of a whirlwind of red, pink, and
purple gel pens, crumpled heart-shaped doilies, and scraps of
mangled construction paper. She stared morosely at her half-
decorated shoebox and tiny stack of crooked Valentines. They
couldn't afford to buy cards at the store this year, so Kimmy had
to try to make them.

All she wanted was to make it a happy Valentine's Day
for everyone. They'd had a rough year in room 204. Half of the
kids' parents had lost their jobs when the factory closed, Mary's
grandma died, and Tabby, Kimmy's best friend, had just lost her
puppy.

Kimmy's parents were upstairs, asleep after long
graveyard shifts at the convenience store and the Wal-Mart. She
almost never saw them anymore.

She just wanted to see everyone smiling again. Just for
one day. Why did she have to be such crap with scissors?

There was only one thing to do now. She crept into her
mother's sewing room and pulled up the loose floorboard in the
corner. She pulled out an undecorated shoebox, heavy with old
photos and clinking glass vials. She dug through the box till she
found the foggy brown glass vial labeled "Happiness," in her
mother's scrawled handwriting.

Kimmy shook it. Liquid sloshed, but it sounded less than
half full. She hoped it would be enough.

She and her mother had made candy for family Christmas

presents this year, and they still had a whole brick of bulk chocolate left.

Kimmy dragged a stool over to the stove and set up a double boiler. She melted half of the chocolate, then added the other half and all that was in the Happiness vial. She poured the melted chocolate into heart-shaped molds and slid them into the fridge.

She only burned herself once.

She went to bed with a smile on her lips.

*

She left her parents each a chocolate heart on the kitchen table, next to their crooked, heart-shaped cards.

She gave everyone in Room 204 a heart, even smelly Jeremy Smallman and old Mrs. Buchnall. She kept one for herself, and there was still one left over.

She gave the extra one to Tabby, who split it with Mary.

The chocolate was sweet and rich, and it tasted like something deeper, too. It reminded her of snowdrops and daffodils poking up through late spring snow, of learning to bake with her mother, of her father carrying her on his shoulders, of sleepovers when Tabby's mom would let them eat ice cream for breakfast.

Happiness bubbled up from Kimmy's belly. She looked around the room, and everyone was grinning. All of their boxes were crammed with homemade Valentines, and Danny, the cutest boy in the class, handed Kimmy her card instead of putting it in her box. "Thanks for the chocolate," he said. "It was great." He blushed and looked at her shoebox. "You're great, too."

*

Kimmy skipped home. She'd done it! She'd given everyone a happy day!

Her mother was waiting for her at the kitchen table. She was looking down at the Happiness vial. "You shouldn't go into my things without asking," she said.

Kimmy stared at the floor. "You were sleeping."

"What did you do with this?" her mother asked.

"I put it in the chocolate hearts for everyone's Valentine's Day present."

Kimmy's mother trailed a finger along her own, uneaten, heart. She handed Kimmy the vial.

It was heavier than it had been. She shook it. "It's full!"

"Happiness grows when it's shared," her mother said.

"Why haven't we been using it, then?" Kimmy asked.

Her mother shrugged. "I was afraid that it wasn't any good anymore. After everything that's happened, I—I guess I was afraid to find out. I'm glad it's still good. I'm proud of you, Kimmy. You did a good thing. Just ask me next time, okay?"

"Okay."

"Come on. Let's make your father a fancy dinner. We should have just enough time."

"Should we add anything? More Happiness? Maybe some Love?" Kimmy asked.

Her mother hugged her. "You add Happiness and Love to everything you touch. You're special like that."

"Oh. Okay." A grin tugged at the edges of Kimmy's lips.

"Happy Valentine's Day, Kimmy."

"Happy Valentine's Day, Mom."

~~~
~~~

A Date with Medusa

Bonus Story

For a while, I was experimenting with publishing short fiction on my website. The following stories are all also available to read online. The myth of Medusa has always interested me, and I've written a few stories loosely inspired by her tale.

She ran the razor over her scalp, feeling lighter and lighter as snakes plopped to the floor. They'd grow back. She'd done this before. She pulled on a stocking cap and a pair of dark sunglasses and went out for coffee.

She flirted with the boy who made her cappuccino, and when his shift was over they went back to her place. She kissed him all over, loving the way his flesh felt next to hers.

"I want to see your eyes." He reached for her glasses.

She grabbed his fingers and shook her head.

"Please." He smiled and touched her cheek. "I'm sure they're beautiful."

She never could resist a compliment. She took off her glasses and felt his hand grow cold and hard against her skin.

She put him in the basement with the others.

~~~
~~~

Prohibited Comfort

I was walking down the sidewalk with my headphones on, and this just came into my head.

A woman in a red sweater stopped in the middle of the sidewalk and started to cry. One second, she was like everyone else, carefully expressionless and plugged in to her headphones, then she burst into noisy tears. People didn't do that. Michael's steps faltered. He wanted to stop, to reach out to her. People didn't do that anymore either.

His girlfriend tugged his arm. Michael took a step toward the crying woman; his eyes met hers. They were blue, like the sky people no longer looked at, like his mother's eyes, the day she was taken away. His girlfriend tugged his arm again. Michael took another step toward the woman, and his girlfriend let him go.

Michael touched the crying woman's shoulder, and she threw herself into his arms. Hot tears soaked through his shirt. He stroked her hair.

When the thought police came, they took both of them.

~~~
~~~

First Time

This was inspired by a challenge from a flash fiction magazine called The Drabbler.

I'm ready to be the first man to make love to an Atareen. Xteela's so exotic, with her blue skin and gold eyes. I begin unwinding the layers of her alien clothing.

She hooks her fingernails into her smooth skin and starts pulling it off, revealing green flesh.

"What are you doing?"

"I'm removing my skin. How can we truly become one with our skin between us?"

"My skin doesn't come off."

"Oh," she croons. "I didn't know that this was your first time. I'll be gentle." She reaches for me, and her fingernails glint razor sharp in the candlelight.

~~~
~~~

Taking Root

Bonus Story

This story appeared in Bards and Sages Quarterly in 2010. It's pretty creepy, and I've always been pretty pleased with it.

Thick black mud squeezed up between Mary's bare toes. She sank deeper into her mother's flower garden, until the tops of her feet were obscured. She wiggled her toes, and the surface of the mud undulated. She imagined roots growing out of her feet, reaching deep into the earth to bring her nutrients.

She could feel her body absorbing energy from the sun.

She looked over to where her mother was weeding. "Look at me, Mommy, I'm turning into a tree!"

"Oh, honey, you're going to get mud all over your pretty new dress," her mother said.

"It doesn't matter. I won't need dresses when I'm a tree."

Her mother sighed and stood up. "Come on, let's get you cleaned up." She wrapped her arms around Mary's waist and pulled.

Mary tried to hold on to the ground with her roots, but her mother was too strong. Sharp pain shot through her feet, and she started to scream. She popped out of the ground.

Her legs ended at the ankle. She felt herself shriveling up, dying like all the other weeds her mother pulled. "I was going to be a tree," she whispered.

~~~
~~~

The Ghost Under the Ice

Bonus Story

This story appeared in Bards and Sages Quarterly in 2009. This is another one that I've always been happy with.

Elisha waited for weeks for the lake to freeze over again. She needed to see if her dreams were true. Her counselor told her that she needed to let go, but how could she when she knew deep down inside that Caitlyn would never abandon her?

Thick snow crunched and thin ice groaned beneath her booted feet. She tested the ice before taking each step.

She reached the center of the lake, where the wind had scoured the snow away, and looked down through the translucent ice. Caitlyn floated beneath her, just like in her dreams, her hands supporting the ice beneath Elisha's feet. Her dark hair, no longer brown, but gray like the winter sky, drifted around her head, and when she smiled her teeth glistened like fish scales.

Elisha lowered herself onto her belly; her twin stretched out with her. Their cheeks and fingertips pressed together on opposite sides of the ice. The movement of water beneath the ice formed words. "You came."

"I'll always come," Elisha said. When her skin started to burn from the cold, Elisha stood up and walked back to the shore, trusting her sister to hold her weight.

~~~
~~~

Her Chosen Path

Martha spotted the point where the rainbow touched the ground and rushed toward it. She promised herself that she'd make it to the end this time. She scrambled up the rainbow's slick surface, slipping back two paces for every three she took.

The colors beneath her thinned, and she ran faster, nearly careening off the narrow path beneath her sliding boots.

The rainbow faded. Martha fell.

She landed in a wet pine forest, on scraping branches and stabbing roots. Pain lanced through her body. She choked on muddy needles and frustrated tears. Cold rain ran down the back of her neck, and dirty water soaked into her boots. She rolled over and wiped her face on her filthy sleeve, and needles scraped her cheeks.

She'd traveled far on the rainbow path—she had no idea where she was. The land around her was strange. The clouds moved toward the unfamiliar mountains that pierced the sky in the distance. The familiar smell of the sea was gone, replaced by the heavy aroma of wet pine and cold mud.

Standing hurt. Walking was worse. She pushed mud-drenched hair out of her face and limped after the rain. *Next time*, she promised herself. *I'll make it next time.*

~~~
~~~

Martian Adventures

Bonus Story

I wrote this as a series of pieces for my website in 2010. I posted a new section every Friday. I'd like to expand Jim and Ronnie's story someday, but for now, I hope you enjoy this slice of their lives.

New Friends

Ronnie waited outside the new boy's cryosleep pod, barely keeping herself from bouncing up and down. She wasn't supposed to be here—Mom had told her to let the new settlers get settled before she started pestering them. But she couldn't wait. She wanted to meet James P. Morgan.

She traced the nameplate on his pod. He was twelve, only two years older than her. Maybe he'd be her friend. She'd never had a friend before.

The pod beeped. Ronnie bit her fingertips. This was it.

The lid hissed open, and James sat up. He was wearing the same gray jumpsuit that Ronnie had on. His short dark hair stuck up in the back, and he was thin and pale from the cryosleep. He blinked at her. "Who are you?"

"I'm Ronnie."

He wrinkled his nose. "That's not a girl's name."

"It's short for Veronica."

"Oh," James said. "I'm Jim."

"I'm very pleased to meet you." Ronnie extended her hand. "Want me to help you out of there?"

Jim's legs were wobbly, and he leaned on Ronnie's shoulder. Joy curled in her belly.

"Are there any other kids here?" Jim asked.

Ronnie shook her head. "Nope. Just me. Just us, now. None of the other scientists have kids. Dr. Marie is pregnant, though."

Jim nodded. "I knew someone was. My dad's excited to deliver the first Martian baby." He looked around the room. "Where is everyone else?"

"All the pods are spread out so that people can get their bearings before they meet anyone." Ronnie blushed and stared at her feet. "I'm not supposed to be here."

"Oh," said Jim. "Well, I'm glad you are. I'd have fallen on my face if not for you."

Ronnie grinned. Jim's balance was getting better, but she didn't want to rush him. It was nice, having someone lean on her. "There's a lot of cool stuff to see," she said. "I know a secret way into the greenhouses."

They reached the hall, and Ronnie's mom spotted them. "There you are! What do you think you're doing! I can't believe you! You've invaded this poor boy's privacy! You're grounded for the next week, young lady."

Ronnie wanted to melt into the floor. Grounded! But she wanted to show Jim around the station!

"I don't mind," Jim said. "Really. I'm glad she was here."

Mom's glare softened. "She really shouldn't have bothered you right after you woke up from cryosleep."

"Please don't ground her, ma'am," he said. "She promised to show me around."

"Well, if you really don't mind, then I suppose I won't ground her. Come on, honey. You've got chores."

Ronnie was grinning so hard that her cheeks hurt. She had a friend.

Into the Greenhouse

James—no, Jim, he had to start thinking of himself as Jim—couldn't believe his luck. The only other kid on Mars was a cute girl. A cute, nice girl who was obviously excited about the idea of being his friend.

No one had ever been excited to be his friend before. He'd never had a nickname before, either, but Ronnie had one, and James—Jim—felt like he should too. She'd already introduced him to everyone on the station as Jim.

Not only was he on a whole new world, but he had a whole new identity.

And good riddance. Good riddance to Earth, and good riddance to James.

Ronnie was taking him to the greenhouses. They were apparently off-limits, but Ronnie knew a way around all of the locked doors.

"It's my favorite place in the whole station," she said, leading him through a series of twists and turns. "When they first decided to start a colony here, they sent robots, and they built the first domes and planted the first trees. They were little, stunted things, engineered to be able to live in the crappy atmosphere and terrible soil. There are only a few of those left, since we're able to grow bigger trees now." Ronnie opened a final door, and stepped into the alien forest.

Red Martian soil crunched beneath Jim's feet, and branches arched overhead, obscuring the oddly-colored sky above the clear dome. The air tasted odd, but it wasn't unpleasant or hard to breathe. "Wow," he said, staring around. "This is incredible."

Ronnie grinned. "There are other greenhouses, too, where we grow food, and most of the oxygen actually comes from the algae tubs, but this," she extended her arms and twirled around. "This is where it all started."

59

"Hey!" a distant voice shouted.

Jim jumped at the unexpected yell, and Ronnie grimaced.

"Crap," she hissed. "We've been spotted. That sounds like Dr. Eric."

"Did I meet him?" Jim asked, edging toward the door. He didn't want to get in trouble. He'd only been here a day.

"Yeah. He was the old guy with the glasses and the funny accent." Ronnie glanced between the tree trunks. "He's a ways off yet. I bet we could outrun him. And he wouldn't rat us out to my mom."

"You want to run? To where?" She was crazy.

Ronnie nodded. "Deeper into the woods. He won't follow us. Come on, Jim!" She took off, dodging around tree trunks. Red dust puffed behind her.

James wouldn't have followed. He would have stayed, listened to a lecture, and then gone home.

But James didn't exist on Mars. Jim sprinted after his friend.

The Hideout

Ronnie loved running, and the forbidden greenhouse was her favorite place to do it. She dodged between trees and glanced back. Jim was following her, and they'd already lost Dr. Eric.

Joy gave her feet wings. She didn't slow down till she got to her hideout. When Jim finally caught up, he was panting and holding his side.

A wave of guilt washed over her. "Oh, Jim, I'm sorry! I forgot that you're not used to our air yet."

Jim shook his head. "It's not the air. I'm not much of a runner."

Ronnie liked how modest he was, and how he tried not to let her feel bad. He was an awesome friend. She couldn't believe how lucky she was. "Well, don't worry. I'll whip you into shape."

"I guess getting me in shape might make up for getting me into trouble," Jim said.

Ronnie blushed. "Dr. Eric really won't tell on us. We won't be in trouble, I promise. Anyway, this is what I wanted to show you." She pointed up into the branches. "This is the tallest tree on Mars."

Jim looked up and whistled. The tree trunk was mammoth, and the branches stretched up to the top of the dome.

"They have to trim it, or else it'd keep growing and break the glass. They take most of the limbs to compost, but they left a few." She led him around the huge base of the tree. "This is my hideout." She'd wrestled gnarled limbs as thick as her waist into a rough teepee and covered them with canvas. The base was wide, but they had to duck through the flap. They couldn't stand inside, but there was room for them both to stretch out on the ground. She'd stashed a canteen, some protein bars, an emergency lamp, and her spare book reader in the middle of the space.

Jim examined the hideout carefully, tracing the grain of the wood and fingering the thick canvas. "It's brilliant."

Ronnie beamed. "It's my special place. It can be our special place, now. I come out here when my mom's driving me crazy."

"It'll be a good place to avoid my dad when he's angry, too," Jim said, idly leafing through her book selection. "I have a bunch of books I could load onto this for you. And I have an old game console I could bring out here. And we could get more water, and a camp stove, or something."

Ronnie listened to him planning, and smiled to herself. Her hideout had a different feel to it when she shared it with a friend. She liked it.

Cafeteria Food

Jim didn't like cafeterias. He'd had bad experiences in cafeterias. Of course, the adult scientists weren't likely to dump chocolate milk on his lap or make fun of him for reading at recess, but he was still uneasy. He stuck close to Ronnie as she got in line.

She was practically bouncing in excitement. "It's pasta day! I love pasta day."

Jim wasn't sure if he'd call it pasta. It was shaped like spaghetti, but it was green and made out of algae. The sauce looked normal though, and it smelled good. Ronnie dished out two intimidating plates of algae pasta and smothered them in tomato sauce.

He'd seen the tomato vines that they'd coaxed into trees in the greenhouses. He'd never realized how many tomatoes one vine could produce.

Ronnie led him to a table and plopped one of the plates down in front of him. "You're going to love it," she promised.

Jim poked the pasta with his fork. It looked like long strands of snot. Ronnie took an enthusiastic bite and closed her eyes in pleasure. Jim glanced around. Everyone else seemed to be enjoying it, too.

He squeezed his eyes shut and took a bite.

"Hey, this is actually pretty good!" he said. It was pleasantly chewy, and had a subtle saltiness that complimented the sauce.

Ronnie nodded as she shoveled food into her mouth. "My mom came up with the recipe," she said. "She's brilliant. Annoying, but brilliant."

"What's her job here?" Jim asked.

"She organizes things. She makes schedules and menus and keeps track of how much food we have and how much we need to plant and all that sort of stuff. She's pretty busy. What's your mom going to do?"

"Oh, she's going to assist my dad. That's what she did back home, too."

"Back on Earth," Ronnie corrected, grinning around a mouthful of green pasta. "Mars is your home now."

"Yeah. Back on Earth," Jim agreed. He cleaned off his plate.

"You want seconds?" Ronnie asked.

After they finished second helpings of pasta, they had green spice cake made with algae flour and honey. Jim was stuffed. He looked around the cafeteria. It wasn't so bad, after all.

After a long, contented sigh, Ronnie pulled him to his feet. "Come on, I want to show you the fish!"

The Fish Tanks

Ronnie leaned out over the fish tank. She'd brought Jim up onto the catwalks over the aquariums. Mom would flip if she saw them up here, but Ronnie liked looking down at the water. The algae tanks were okay, but the fish were the best. Their silver scales flickered as they darted back and forth.

"Aren't they awesome?" Ronnie asked. "They're genetically modified trout. We use the whole fish. Anything that we don't eat gets composted."

Jim mirrored her pose, leaning over the railing and looking straight down. "They really are pretty—oh crap!" His foot slipped, and Jim pitched forward. Ronnie made a frantic grab for his legs, but she missed, and he tumbled off of the catwalk into the water below. The fish scattered.

Ronnie screamed. She'd had a best friend for all of a week, and she'd managed to drown him. "Jim!" She sprinted down the catwalk and scrambled down the ladder, calling his name, barely keeping from sobbing. Tears blurred her vision as she wove around other tanks to get to where Jim had fallen.

She ran to the side of the tank, expecting to see him thrashing around as he died, or, even worse, his dead eyes gazing back at her. Instead, he climbed over the edge of the tank and dropped down beside her, soaked, but alive.

Ronnie threw herself into his arms. "You're okay! I was so afraid—I was sure you'd drown."

Jim hugged her and patted her back. "It's okay. I'm fine."

"Why didn't you tell me that you could swim?" Ronnie asked, wiping away tears and laughing from pure relief.

"It didn't come up." Jim raked his wet hair out of his eyes. "Can't you?"

"No. These tanks are the only places on the planet with enough water to swim in, and I'm not supposed to be here."

Jim laughed. "Do you ever go anywhere that you're

supposed to be?"

Ronnie wrinkled her nose. "I'm only supposed to be at home, studying, or at the cafeteria, eating. I'm not allowed to go anywhere cool."

Jim grinned and shook his head. He was still holding her, and she was getting soaked. She stepped back. "Come on, we need to sneak back and change before anyone sees how wet we are."

"Good idea," Jim said.

They climbed back up onto the catwalk and made their way to the hallway access.   "Jim?" Ronnie said.

"Yeah?"

"I'm glad you can swim."

"Me too." Jim said.

"Maybe someday, you could teach me."

"Yeah," he said. "I'd like that."

Family Day

Jim scowled at his book reader. He hated Sundays. Ronnie's dad had declared Sundays "Family Days" and so Ronnie was trapped with her mom and dad doing family crap. Ronnie said it wasn't too bad, and that she'd try to get her dad to let him come over sometime.

Jim's dad was at his office. He didn't take days off. Days off were for the weak, and quality family time was a waste of his talents.

Jim flopped back on his bed and sighed. Before Mars, spending a Sunday alone wouldn't have been a problem. He would have been perfectly happy to just read, maybe watch a vid or two, play some video games. But he couldn't concentrate. He kept imagining Ronnie and her parents, laughing together, playing board games, or baking or something.

Jim went to go find his mom. She was in the kitchen, making sandwiches. Hydroponic tomatoes and dried trout on algae bread. "James," she said, giving him a little smile.

"Hey, Mom, I was wondering if you wanted to do something. Maybe play some scrabble."

"Oh, honey, that'd be lovely, but your father wants me to head over to the lab to help him."

"Oh. Okay," Jim said.

"Maybe we can play when I get back," his mother said, slipping the sandwiches into a lunchbox. "We shouldn't be more than a couple of hours."

Jim shook his head. "Nah. Don't worry about it. I think I'll go for a walk."

His mom looked down at the table. "Do you want me to make you a sandwich?"

Jim shook his head again. "I'll get something at the cafeteria."

"Okay. Love you, James. I'll see you for dinner."

Jim watched her walk down the hall toward his father's lab, and turned the other way. "It's Jim, Mom," he muttered.

He wandered aimlessly, his feet automatically taking him down the now-familiar paths, until a voice shouted, "Hey!"

Jim froze. Was this one of the places where he wasn't supposed to be? Almost everywhere Ronnie took him seemed to be out-of-bounds. He turned and prepared himself for a lecture.

A maintenance engineer waved him over. Jim thought Ronnie had introduced him, but he couldn't remember his name. "You're Jim, right?"

Jim's stomach sank as he nodded. The engineer was going to tell his parents.

"I'm Don." He held out his hand, and Jim shook it, confused.

"You busy?" Don asked.

"Not really," Jim said.

"Want to give me a hand with this?" He nodded to a pump that he was fixing. "Hold this while I tighten this over here."

Jim did as he asked, and Don thanked him. "Can I help you with anything else?" Jim asked.

"Sure." Don handed him a toolbox. "We're always short staffed on Sundays."

Jim spent the next four hours helping Don. He squirmed into spaces where Don's wide shoulders didn't fit, handed him tools, and held things steady. The whole time, Don explained everything that he was doing, step by step.

Jim forgot all about Family Day, and absorbed Don's lessons like a sponge. He'd always been fascinated by mechanical things, but his father said that manual labor was beneath him.

Don wiped his hands on his pants, leaving greasy streaks. He glanced at his watch. "I'd better let you go, or you're going to miss dinner. I really appreciated your help, today."

Jim's stomach rumbled, and he remembered that he'd missed lunch. "Would you mind if I came back next Sunday?" he asked.

"That'd be great, Jim." Don grinned. "Thanks again. See you in a week."

Jim managed to get home and shower before his parents got home from the lab. He was looking forward to next Sunday.

*

Ronnie scowled at her blueberry pancakes. "I don't see why Jim can't come over."

Her parents exchanged a look. Her dad arched an eyebrow, and her mom shook her head. Ronnie sighed, knowing the answer, even before Dad turned to her. "It's family day, Ronnie," he said. "It's a day for just the three of us. You can see Jim every other day of the week."

Ronnie sighed and poked at her breakfast. She'd wanted to see Jim's reaction to her mom's pancakes. He told her that he'd never seen green pancakes before. It would be so strange to live on Earth, where flour was white. It'd make the food look so boring.

"I guess it's okay," she said finally. "His parents probably want to spend time with him, too."

Her parents exchanged another look, then her mom clapped her hands together. "Let's get this table cleared away, and then we can get suited up and head out."

"Can I take Jim outside the dome sometime, Dad? Not on a family day?"

"Sure, pumpkin," Dad said. "As long as his parents don't mind."

"His parents won't mind." Ronnie felt wistful envy of Jim's lack of supervision. He said that his parents didn't care what he did, as long as it didn't make them look bad. Her parents wanted to know where she was every minute of every day.

"I'm sure they won't," Mom said. She used the tone she normally reserved for Earth politicians during funding cuts. She dumped a load of plates in the sink. "Come on. Let's go hiking."

Dad helped Ronnie into her suit. She didn't need his help, but he would insist on double checking if she did it on her own, and that'd take twice as long. She wanted to get outside.

The tan sky stretched overhead, and the red dirt crunched beneath her boots. Her own breath was loud in her ears. Her mom took her left hand, and her dad took her right, and they went hiking. They liked the winding path that went up the Cliffside behind the dome. They'd get to the top and look down on it. Ronnie's dad said that it helped to put their world in perspective.

After their hike, Ronnie and Dad made dinner. It was the only meal of the week that Mom didn't have to think about. They usually burnt it, but Ronnie thought that they were getting better.

Then they played scrabble. She couldn't wait till tomorrow, when she could tell Jim all about it.

Exploration

Jim examined the spacesuit. It didn't look at all like the ones in the vids about the history of spaceflight. It looked more like the wetsuit that he'd worn when his grandmother took him SCUBA diving. It was sleek and black and rubbery against his fingers.

Ronnie was already wearing hers. "Hurry up!" she urged. "We've only got a few more hours of daylight."

Jim was nervous about leaving the dome. Excited, too. He read the directions posted next to the suits again, then followed them carefully, step by step. Ronnie tapped her foot. She was practically bouncing up and down with excitement. They'd been busy with school for weeks—their computerized teachers insisted on giving them midterms—and she'd been going crazy waiting to show him the planet.

Jim had aced his midterms. Ronnie, with his help studying, had done better than she ever had before. Her mom had made him a thank-you cake.

Jim pulled the helmet over his head and heard it click solidly into place. The suits were well maintained—he knew because he'd helped service them a few weeks ago.

"Finally! Okay, now, we check each other, make sure everything's fastened and zipped and everything." Ronnie scanned him. "Looks good."

Jim took longer examining Ronnie's suit, but it was perfect, too. "Okay." He took a deep breath. "Let's go."

They cycled through the airlock, and Jim took his first steps into the thin Martian air. He couldn't feel heat or cold through his suit, but he could hear the squeaky crunch his boots made as they sank into the dusty ground.

The sky overhead was the color of butterscotch pudding, and his external microphone picked up the distant keening of the wind.

Jim almost staggered under the reality of actually standing on another planet. Being inside the station wasn't that different from being inside anywhere, really, but here—it was just so alien. He longed for blue sky, open water, stands of trees, swaths of green grass. Instead, it was all barren rocks and dust as far as the eye could see.

He looked over at Ronnie, who was grinning. "Isn't it beautiful?" She grabbed his hand. "Come on, there's a great view of the whole station from up on that cliff."

She hadn't been born on Mars, but she didn't remember Earth. She had no concept of what Jim was missing. She'd never felt a natural breeze on her bare skin. Jim might never step foot on Earth again.

Her fingers laced through his, padded by their suits. "Come on, Jim. Let me show you our planet."

He squeezed her hand and tried to tell himself that giving up Earth was worth it.

*

Ronnie stopped a few feet away from the edge of the cliff. "Look. Isn't it amazing?"

Jim stood next to her and stared down at the station. "It really stands out, doesn't it? Especially the dome. The greenhouses might be the only green on the whole planet."

Ronnie had never thought about there being green anywhere else. "I guess."

"Where to now?" Jim asked.

"What do you mean?" Ronnie asked.

"Where are we going next? We've explored one path, looked down on the station, what's next?"

Ronnie frowned. "There is no next. This is the only path I know. We only come up here."

"Well, let's wander off the path, then. It's not like we can really get lost. We can see the station for miles, and there's a display that shows how far away and what direction it's in built into our suits."

"You've got your helmet display on?" Ronnie asked. She always turned hers off. She hated how it cluttered up her field of vision.

"It's a safety feature." Jim took a few steps off the path. "Come on."

Ronnie followed him. She didn't like this. Jim was always the responsible one. The one who made sure she did her homework before they goofed off. He shouldn't be the one gallivanting off of the path.

Jim took a few steps more, then the ground opened up under his feet, and he plunged into a hole. His yelp of surprise echoed in her helmet.

Ronnie ran forward, then froze a few feet away from the hole. The edges didn't look stable. "Jim?" she called. Why was he always falling into things?

"I'm okay!"

Ronnie winced. "You don't have to shout, the speaker is still right by my ear."

"Right. Sorry."

Ronnie could just see him in the darkness below. He stood up and looked around, and the faint light reflected on his helmet. "This is awesome. I had no idea that there were caves on Mars."

"It's not safe. It could collapse on you at any second." Ronnie took half a step forward. "We have to call for help."

Jim looked up at her. "Don't you want to come down and look around first?" he asked.

"No. It's not safe, Jim. We need to get you out of there."

He held his arms up. "I can catch you. It's not that far."

Terror churned in her belly as she looked down into the cave. It was so dark. "I'm scared Jim. Please, let's just call for help."

"It'll be okay, Ronnie. Trust me."

She took a deep breath and jumped.

*

Jim staggered a little under Ronnie's weight, but he made sure she landed gently. She felt solid in his arms. He liked it. And they'd held hands, for a bit, too. Did it count as holding hands through their suits? Did this count as a hug?

Probably not. Ronnie liked him as a friend, but he didn't think she liked him like that. Maybe she would someday.

"It's so dark down here," she whispered. She fumbled with something on her glove, and it started to glow. Ronnie sighed. "That's better."

The rock around them was reddish gray, and passages opened up in three directions. Two were too small to explore, but the third looked promising. It was a tall, narrow slit, and Jim thought they could squeeze through. Jim looked at his own gloves. "How do you get them to light up?"

Ronnie eagerly took his hands and pressed buttons just below his middle fingers. More light flooded the chamber. Jim touched the wall, and his glove came away dusty. "It's so dry. The caves I went in with my grandma were always damp." He turned around, examining every nook and cranny. "We're the first human beings to see this, ever." He grinned at Ronnie. "Isn't it amazing?"

Ronnie was looking up at the hole he'd fallen through. It was a few feet above her head. "I guess. How are we going to get out?"

"I'll boost you out, then you'll probably have to call for help to get me out. But stop worrying about it." He'd have her call Don. His parents didn't have to know about this. "Come on, don't you want to see what's around that corner?"

Ronnie glanced down the biggest passage. "What if it collapses on us?"

"It's not going to collapse on us."

"The ceiling gave way where you stepped on it," Ronnie said.

"There isn't anyone else walking around up there," Jim pointed out. "Plus, see how the ceiling gets lower? It's much thicker everywhere else. I stepped on the weakest point. This cave has been her for a long time. We're okay. Really."

"I'm still afraid, Jim. Even if it doesn't make sense to be scared. I don't like it."

Jim blinked. Ronnie was afraid of caves? That was strange. She wasn't afraid of getting yelled at, or disappointing her parents, or of people not liking her, but caves freaked her out? Jim squeezed her shoulder. "Everyone gets scared sometimes, Ronnie. You jumped down here, even though it scared you. That's really brave. We'll just go down to the next corner, and if you're still don't like it, we'll come right back. I promise."

Ronnie took a deep breath. "Okay."

Jim led her through the twisting passage, careful never to get too far ahead. He reached the first turn and squeezed around it. "Oh, wow." The cave opened up in front of him to a huge chamber. The ground fell away a few feet away into a massive chasm. He couldn't see the bottom. "Ronnie, you have to see this."

Ronnie gasped. "It's huge," she said.

"It reminds me of the Grand Canyon, back on Earth." He took Ronnie's hand and squeezed it. "I wonder if we just found evidence for running water here on Mars."

The Valor Crevasse

Ronnie still couldn't get over how everyone had reacted to their discovery. The geology department gave both her and Jim specially created paperweights carved out of Martian rock and had thrown them a party. The engineers had started designing robots to explore the crevasse. Her mom had dedicated a whole week of menus to Ronnie and Jim's favorite foods.

And her dad insisted that she and Jim name the crevasse. He'd suggested the Morgan/Barrie Crevasse, but Ronnie didn't think Jim would like that. He wouldn't want his father's name attached to their discovery.

She didn't even think he'd told his dad. He'd blushed all through the geology department party, but he'd looked happy, except when anyone asked about his dad. But most people didn't ask. Jim wasn't the only one who didn't like Dr. Morgan.

Ronnie stared up at her ceiling. She needed to think of a good name. One that she could suggest to Jim that'd make his face light up. He always lit up when he really loved one of her ideas.

He was so cute when he smiled.

She'd been so afraid in the cave, and he'd been so understanding and encouraging.

Valor. She'd suggest that they call it The Valor Crevasse. She jumped out of bed and ran to her computer console. She called Jim. "Hey."

Jim grinned at her through the console. He was wearing his headphones. Ronnie wondered if he'd been listening to music or playing a game. "What's up, Ronnie?"

"I came up with an idea for what to name the crevasse."

Jim ran a hand through his hair and left it standing straight up. "Is your dad still going on about that?"

"I think we should call it The Valor Crevasse."

Jim's face lit up. "That's brilliant, Ronnie."

"I'm glad you like it. I'll go tell dad."

"Right. I'll see you tomorrow in class, then. Night, Ronnie."

After Jim signed off, Ronnie replayed the last few minutes of the video. She saved it before she went downstairs.

The Naming Ceremony

Jim stuffed his tie in his pocket. Ronnie's mom could help him with it. He crept out of his room and into the dark kitchen. Just a few more steps, and he'd be out.

"James?" His mom flicked the light on. "What are you doing up this early? And why are you wearing a suit?"

Jim ran his hand through his hair. "I've got to go to a thing."

"A thing," his mom repeated. "What kind of thing?"

"A naming ceremony," Jim muttered. He hadn't wanted to explain this to his parents.

"A naming ceremony? I don't understand. The baby was born months ago."

"Not for the baby. For a crevasse that Ronnie and I found."

"A crevasse?"

"The geologists are arguing about whether it's proof of running water on Mars, or proof of some weird volcanic activity."

"You and your friend made some sort of major discovery, and you didn't tell me about it?"

Jim sighed. She sounded hurt. "I didn't want to bother you."

His mom sat down in one of the kitchen chairs. Her lips were pressed together in a white line. "I see."

"You and Dad have been so busy, and I knew that he wouldn't care."

"I'm not your father," she snapped. "I care."

Jim looked at his watch. "It starts in half an hour. I'm meeting Ronnie and her parents in five minutes."

His mom stood. "James, I'd like to come, if you don't

mind. I can get dressed and meet you at Ronnie's."

"Of course I don't mind, Mom. And I can wait. I'll let Ronnie know." He pulled the tie out of his pocket. "Could you tie this for me?"

His mom's face lit up. "Of course, honey."

"And Mom? It's Jim, now."

*

Mrs. Morgan looked taller without Jim's dad towering over her. And she looked pretty in her pink-flower dress and pearls. And Jim looked very solemn in his suit. Ronnie grinned and waved. Jim waved back.

Ronnie's mom had redecorated the cafeteria for the ceremony. The tables had been stashed somewhere, and the chairs were lined up facing the front of the room. Dark blue drapes concealed the kitchen. Ronnie and Jim both had chairs up at the front, behind the podium. Ronnie adjusted the chairs so that they were perfectly parallel.

Jim led his mom over to Ronnie and her parents. The adults shook hands, then Jim's mom turned to Ronnie. "I hear congratulations are in order, Veronica."

"No one calls her that, Mom," Jim whispered.

His mom's smile looked pained, and Ronnie took her hand. "It's okay, Mrs. Morgan. You can call me either Veronica or Ronnie, whichever you like."

Jim's mom squeezed Ronnie's fingers. "Both are very nice names, but if everyone else calls you Ronnie, I guess I should, too."

"Thanks, Mrs. Morgan. I like your dress. It's very pretty."

Jim and his mom both blushed, but they looked pleased. "Jim helped me pick it."

Jim's cheeks got even redder. "Mom!"

"It's nice to see you out of uniform, Mrs. Morgan," Ronnie's mom said. "I don't think I've seen you in anything but scrubs since you got here!"

"Well, Charles does keep me busy." Mrs. Morgan glanced at Jim, then down at the floor.

"Dad's work is very important to him," Jim said, also looking at the floor.

Ronnie fought to keep a scowl off her face. She'd known that Jim's dad made him miserable, but she hadn't realized that he made Jim's mom miserable, too. She wondered if Jim realized.

"Well, work is great, but people need recreation to really stay sharp," Ronnie said. Her parents smiled at her. "And I think you should take some time off and come over for dinner sometime."

"That would be great," Ronnie's dad said.

Ronnie knew that her parents would back her. They had moments of being completely awesome.

"Dad doesn't like eating with other people," Jim said.

"Well, he doesn't have to come, does he?" Ronnie asked.

"No. He doesn't," Mrs. Morgan said. "I think dinner sounds lovely. Thank you for the invitation, Ronnie."

Jim gaped at her. "Really? You're willing to go without dad?"

"I'm not your father, Jam—Jim," she said.

The cafeteria had filled up as they talked. "Maybe we'd better find seats," Ronnie's mom said. "You two go ahead and sit down. We'll get the ceremony started in a minute."

Ronnie's parents each squeezed one of her shoulders, and Jim's mom kissed his cheek. Everyone found their seats, and the ceremony began.

*

Jim zoned out a little during the speeches. He listened while Ronnie's dad got up and talked for a while about the purpose of the colony—about exploration and the indomitable human spirit. It was the same sort of thing that Ronnie's dad

80

always went on about. Jim's lips twitched. He really liked Ronnie's dad. But the scientist's speeches about what the crevasse could mean got a little tedious.

He glanced at his mom. She was still there. He could barely believe that his dad hadn't called her away for something. Maybe things really were changing.

She saw him looking at her and beamed at him.

Finally, it was time for his speech. He looked out over the crowd of friendly faces. He spotted Don in the back.

Jim's knees shook. He'd tried to get out of this, but Ronnie had insisted.

The crazy girl thought that speeches were fun. Jim hoped that he wouldn't embarrass himself too badly.

"When my dad decided to bring my family to Mars, I wasn't sure what to think. We've always moved a lot, but I'd never even thought about leaving the Earth behind.

"The year before we left, my grandmother took me on a whirlwind tour of the planet. She wanted to convince me to stay with her. That didn't happen, but I did get to see some amazing things on Earth.

"But I've seen some amazing things on Mars, too. Ronnie and I were the first two humans to see the Valor Crevasse. Standing there, looking at it was one of the most amazing feelings I've ever had. There aren't many new places to find on Earth.

"But my favorite thing about Mars is the people. There's an incredible sense of community in this colony. You've all made me feel welcome from the moment I opened my eyes here, and I want to thank you for that.

"And most of all, I want to thank Ronnie. She's the best friend I've ever had, and without her, I never would have had the courage to wander off of the path, and the Valor Crevasse would still be unknown."

Applause thundered around him. His mom's cheeks were wet. Ronnie squeezed his hand. "Told you speeches are fun."

Moms

Ronnie curled up in the hideout and pulled out one of the chocolate bars that Jim's grandma had sent with him. They didn't get much chocolate on Mars, and Ronnie usually savored it.

She devoured the bar in four bites. Her mom was driving her crazy. She thought that she knew more than Ronnie did about Jim and his dad, and she was just wrong. And Jim didn't want her mom's help dealing with it. He'd been dealing with it all of his life. He was fine.

Ronnie pressed her hands over her eyes. How could one person be so embarrassing? She'd practically smothered Jim with affection, and it was plain to anyone with eyes that it was all fake. Her mom liked Jim well enough, but she hadn't really paid much attention to him before she'd gotten all buddy-buddy with Jim's mom.

Now she oozed sympathy every time Jim's name was mentioned, and it made Ronnie's skin crawl.

Jim ducked into the hideout. "Hey," he said, sitting down next to her.

Ronnie sighed. "I'm so sorry about my mom."

Jim shrugged. "It's okay. A little weird, but not bad. Your mom's just nice. And it's good that she and my mom are friends now. My mom needs friends."

"Yeah, but you're my friend, and she's just... ugh." Ronnie curled her fingers in her hair. "She's driving me nuts."

"That's just how moms are. Don't worry about it." He grinned at her. "So, since I've been helping with maintenance, I've learned a few new shortcuts around the station. Want to go check them out?"

"Okay." Ronnie pushed her mom out of her mind and stood up.

"Come on, I'll race you to the door," Jim called, already running.

Ronnie chased after him, laughing.

He was getting faster—she only beat him by a couple of seconds.

Jim's Birthday

Jim whistled as he walked to work. It was a beautiful Sunday morning, and it was his birthday. He'd been on the station for almost a year. He was going to work a short shift, and then Ronnie, her parents, and his mom were going to throw him a surprise party.

No one had ever tried to throw him a surprise party before. He almost wished that he hadn't overheard his mom and his best friend plotting.

The maintenance staff's break room was dark. Jim usually wasn't the first one in, but when he was it was his job to make coffee. Humming, he flipped the light switch.

"Surprise!" Half the station was crammed into the room. Jim gaped. Don and the rest of the crew grinned at him from behind a cake. Ronnie parents huddled together behind a camera.

Ronnie threw her arms around him. "We totally got you!"

His mom kissed the top of his head. "You should have seen the look on your face!"

"But—I—you—"

"Thought the party was going to be later?" Ronnie said.

Jim nodded.

"That was a diversion." Ronnie pulled him toward the green cake. "It was your mom's idea."

"It was my mom's idea to have cake for breakfast?"

"Yep."

Don slid a generous slice of cake onto a plate. "We got you something," he said, handing Jim a package.

"Go on, open it," urged one of the other maintenance men.

Jim peeled back the plain brown paper. Inside were three workshirts with the station's logo and his name neatly embroidered on them.

"We figured it was about time we made your position official," Don said.

Jim throat felt tight. He nodded and traced his name. "Thanks."

Ronnie pressed a heavy package into his hand. "I got you something, too," she said.

Jim unwrapped it carefully. "Oh, wow, Ronnie." It was three books. One contained all of the technical readouts on the station. Another book, this one on the history of the station and the Mars Project, was tucked behind it. The last was a worn copy of a pulp science fiction novel.

Jim hadn't been able to bring many of his paper books to the station, and he's missed having them on shelves around his room. He didn't even remember mentioning it to Ronnie. The paperback smelled like rainy afternoons at his grandmother's house. "Thank you," he managed.

Ronnie kissed his cheek. "Happy birthday, Jim."

"My best one ever," he said.

"Your best one yet," Ronnie said.

Jim pulled on one of his shirts and took a bite of cake. "Yet," he said.

Ronnie's Birthday

Ronnie wormed her way through the air vent. It was a lot tighter than she remembered—but then she hadn't been through here since before Jim came. She'd grown in the past year.

She slithered forward. It would be her birthday soon, and she always greeted her birthday from the same spot. Of course, she hadn't always had to crawl through vents to get there. The station had grown, too.

She got wedged in a corner. Her legs were tangled together, and it was hard to breathe. She was almost desperate enough to call for help when she managed to get herself unstuck. She patted her wrist communicator. Jim had made it for her and given it to her early. He'd been so excited and proud of himself. He'd never made a present for a friend before.

It was programmed with three settings. One went straight to Jim's matching communicator, the second went to the station's main communication line, and the third was the emergency line.

Jim was a little obsessed with safety. He'd be horrified when she told him about her trip through the vents. She grinned and pictured the look on his face.

She could see sunlight ahead. She was almost there. Just a little further. She pulled herself to the end of the vent. The thin metal shifted beneath her, and the bolts holding the vent moaned.

Ronnie tried to throw herself forward, but her foot caught. She scrambled for something to hold onto as the vent pulled away from the wall. Her stomach lurched, and she started to fall.

She hit her wrist communicator and screamed Jim's name.

*

Ronnie's scream echoed in Jim's room. He grabbed his communicator. "Ronnie? Ronnie, are you okay? Where are you?"

Static crackled at him.

Jim shook the communicator, then tried again. Worry clawed at his belly. Where was she? What had she done?

Maybe this was all a prank. Maybe she was safe, at home, in bed, giggling at him. Still in his pajamas, he ran to Ronnie's house and pounded on the door.

After a few moments, her father came to the door. "Jim, do you know what time it is? What's going on?"

"Is Ronnie here?"

"Of course she is. Go back to bed, Jim."

"Could you check on her? Please?"

Ronnie's dad sighed. "Did you have a bad dream, son?"

Jim shrugged. "I hope so."

Ronnie's dad waved him into the kitchen, then disappeared down the hall. He came back a moment later, and his face was white. "She's gone."

Jim shook his communicator and tried it again. "Ronnie? Ronnie, please answer me."

*

Ronnie groaned. Was that Jim? He sounded far away. "Ronnie! Where are you?"

Thoughts slipped through Ronnie's mind, slippery and hard to catch, like fish. Something was wrong, she was sure of that. She tried to rub her forehead.

Pain exploded through her body. Her arm was wedged beneath her and twisted at a strange angle. Jim's voice was muffled by her back.

"I'm in a ventilation shaft." Ronnie said, remembering. It was her birthday. She stared to cry. "Jim?"

"Ronnie," Jim's voice sounded rough, like he'd been shouting or crying, or both. "You're awake."

"I think my arm's broken," Ronnie said. The ventilation shaft was dark, and the walls were too close together. She couldn't get enough air.

Ronnie could hear her father swearing in the background.

"Which ventilation shaft are you in?"

"I was... going to the observation post." Ronnie was gasping for breath. Everything hurt, and the walls just kept getting closer.

"Calm down, Ronnie. You're going to be okay. I'll find you."

Jim's voice was starting to sound far away again. Ronnie's eyes slipped closed, and his words slipped away.

*

Jim's communicator went silent again, and he spat one of Mr. Barrie's curses. "Where's the observation post?"

Ronnie's dad raked his hands through his thinning hair. "It's in an old part of the station. It's sealed off. There shouldn't be any way in."

"Well, she's in a ventilation shaft. One of them must lead into the sealed off part, right?" Jim asked.

Mr. Dad nodded. "Yeah, but I don't know which one."

"Do you have the station schematics?" Jim asked, thankful that he'd learned how to read them.

Ronnie's dad nodded. He opened them up on his computer, then turned the screen so Jim could see. "The observation post is here." He tapped a tiny room. "It looks like there's only one air vent. It's pretty small, and it hasn't been maintained since we sealed that part of the station off. It must have collapsed under her weight."

Jim traced the ventilation shaft. "I'll go in after her."

"Jim, if it didn't hold her weight, it won't hold yours."

"These sections—the blue ones—should be strong enough. They're reinforced. These red ones are where things'll get dangerous. But we don't have any other choice. I'm not that much bigger than her, and I've spent time in the ventilation shafts before. And I'm still lighter than any of the maintenance robots. I can get her out, Mr. Barrie. I know I can."

Mr. Barrie stared at him for a long moment, then nodded. "I should make you wake your mother, get your parents' permission."

"I'll go get some ropes and a safety harness." Jim ran before Ronnie's dad could change his mind. Ronnie needed him.

*

Ronnie heard Jim's voice, and it made her feel safe. Of course he'd come for her. He'd make everything better. He always did. Her whole life was better than it'd ever been before he came.

She'd read about friends before, watched people in vids, daydreamed about what having someone her age who understood her and liked her and accepted her and didn't care about what she did when she grew up. But Jim was better than any daydream she'd ever had.

And he had such pretty eyes. And soft hair. He chewed his lower lip when he thought about things and blushed whenever someone said something nice about him.

He was just so good. And he was coming for her, all she had to do was hold on. The voices kept telling her that, and she believed them.

Warm hands touched her, and she realized just how cold she'd been. She forced her eyes open. The pain that had ebbed to a background ache flared up, and she whimpered. Jim's face was barely visible behind the glare of the light that was strapped to his forehead.

"Ronnie, Ronnie, come on. Say something."

His hands were so warm. How had she never noticed that before? She smiled at him. "Jim."

Jim touched her cheek. "You're freezing."

Ronnie managed a nod. "S'cold."

"How do you feel about getting out of here?"

"S'my birthday."

"Happy birthday, Ronnie." Jim grabbed her by the

shoulders and pulled her straight up. Ronnie screamed as her weight lifted from her broken arm. She fought to stay conscious, but the pain battered at her senses, and Jim's worried face slipped away.

*

Jim wriggled through the air vents, tugging Ronnie along with him. The vents groaned under their weight, and Jim could hear his heart pounding in his ears even over Ronnie's ragged breathing. Sweat trickled down his nose.

He'd never been more terrified. He was pretty sure that Ronnie's arm was broken, and dragging her through the vents couldn't be doing it any good.

And the vents had collapsed under her weight, so it was a miracle that they were holding up under both of them.

He kept moving, one painful crawling lurch at a time.

"How're you doing, son?" Ronnie's dad's voice made him jump. How could he sound so calm? Maybe it was a grown up thing.

"I'm okay, sir. Ronnie's still out cold." Jim was proud that his voice didn't shake.

"We're tracking you. You're almost out. You're doing great, Jim."

"Thanks, sir."

Jim saw light ahead, and pushed his exhausted body just a little faster. He tumbled out of the air vent, straight into Ronnie's dad's arms. Ronnie slid after him, and her dad caught her, too.

For a second, he just held them. "Thank you," Ronnie's dad breathed, his voice breaking a little.

Then, Jim's dad was pulling Ronnie away. He scowled at Jim. "Her arm's a mess."

"He saved her life," Ronnie's dad said. "We never would have found her if it weren't for Jim."

Jim's dad just rolled his eyes as he rummaged in his bag, and something in Jim snapped. "Nothing I ever do is going to be good enough for you, is it?"

His dad sighed. "You could be good enough, James. If you stopped slacking off and running around with people who are beneath you." His eyes flicked from Ronnie, to her dad, to Don, who was examining the air vent.

"Screw you, Dad. You don't know anything about me, and you don't know anything about anyone else on this station. You think you're so much better than everyone, but you're wrong. You're not better than anyone, Dad. You're not better than Ronnie, or Don, or Mom, or me."

His dad gave Ronnie a shot, then set her arm and sealed a FastHeal cast around it. "You shouldn't talk to your father like that, James." His voice was low and dangerous, but for the first time that he could remember, Jim wasn't afraid of him.

"You've never been a father to me," Jim said.

"I brought you to this planet, James. I support both you and your mother. You're nothing without me. Don't test my patience."

Ronnie's dad put his hand on Jim's shoulder. "Jim's been helping with maintenance, and your wife works as your assistant. They both pull their own weight."

Jim's dad stood up. "You can take your daughter home. She'll need fluids when she wakes up. Come, James. We're going home."

Ronnie's dad's hand tightened on Jim's shoulder. "You can come with us, if you'd rather."

Jim nodded. "I would." He walked away from his father, and he didn't look back.

~~~
~~~

Journal of an Artist

Final Bonus Story

This story appeared in A Fly in Amber. It's not flash, but lots of people liked it, so I figured I'd share it with you.

April 9

The angels watch over us. Everyone knows that. It's their job—it's why they built them.

The angels are beautiful. I like to watch them fly, with the sunlight glittering off of their gold or silver wings. They look like people, from what I can tell, but bigger. I don't know if anyone else notices them. I saw one with bronze wings once, but when I told my keepers about it, none of them believed me. I think it's special—different from the rest of its kind—like me.

I'm training to be an Artist. There are only two dozen of us in the world. We're national treasures. The breeding programs that the government instated in the late 23rd century did an incredible job helping humanity to be more resilient, attractive, and longer-lived, but with the decreased importance of love and individuality, creativity foundered. Within three generations, there were no Artists. So, the government set out to bring us back.

At least that's what they tell me.

My genetic code is a combination of some of the greatest artists of the 22nd century. I started singing and playing the piano at three. I started painting and writing music at six. My first exhibition is this week. I'm not allowed to go. I'm not allowed to meet people. I'm not sure if it's because they're worried that seeing the mundane world will fill me with banality or if they just want to keep me lonely.

But I'm not lonely when I watch the angels. The government made them too. They stop crime. I guess there was less of a public outcry about constant surveillance once they proposed making the machines look like creatures out of Christian mythology. It's sort of funny that all of the religions have gone, but the angels are still here.

I like this journal. Real paper is so rare; I know that they went through a lot of trouble to get it for me. And they promised not to read it. But I don't know if I want to be a writer, too. I already feel a little overwhelmed.

*

April 12

My exhibition was a success. One of my keepers brought me in a clipping from a newspaper that raved about my work. It said my paintings were "inspired and moving." I guess I'm happy about it, even though I'm not sure if my paintings are "inspired and moving" or not. I'm starting to wonder what the point is.

*

April 13

I wish they'd bring my pieces back so I could look at them again, but they sold them all already. I can look at pictures of them, but it's not the same. The pictures don't move me at all. I don't know if looking at the real paintings would be better, or if all Artists feel let down by their own work.

*

April 18

I wish I knew my keepers' names. They know my name. It doesn't seem fair. I mean, they're people, aren't they? And I'm a person, too. Maybe if I knew their names they could be my friends instead of my keepers. Maybe that's why I'm not allowed to know.

*

April 20

I snuck out to the roof to watch the angels. I've never been out at night before. I thought there'd be stars, but I can't see any, even through the gaps in the clouds. The clouds are a horrible color of orange-pink from reflecting all of the lights, but even though it's ugly light, it's enough to see by. At least I can see the moon. I never realized that it was so tiny. Of course, I know it's not full, so it gets bigger. But still.

The angels are so close that I can almost see their faces. I wonder if they can taste the clouds. I wonder what the clouds feel like. I hope they feel nicer than they look.

I want to see an angel up close! I want to paint one. I want to know what it's like to touch one. Are they soft or hard? Warm or cold? Do their feathers feel as smooth and metallic as they look? What color are their eyes? What noises do they make? Do they make machine sounds or human sounds or no sounds at all?

It's windy and cold and it smells bad up here. I wish we had a garden on our roof. The building next door has one. If it wasn't all encased in glass I might be able to smell the flowers. I've never smelled a flower.

How do they expect me to be creative if I've never even smelled a flower?

*

May 1

I just read an article about a woman who claimed that an angel saved her from drowning. No one believed her, because angels don't save people, they only arrest criminals. I think her angel and my angel might be the same. I hope so, even though the article didn't mention the angel's wings being bronze. If I was drowning and an angel came to save me, I don't know if I'd notice the color of its wings. Even if I did no one would believe me, so maybe she just didn't mention it.

I think an angel who saves people is much better than an angel who arrests them.

*

May 5

I finished my latest painting today, and one of my keepers came in and looked at it. I was really proud of it. It's a

94

landscape, a combination of things I've seen in old works and photographs and something I see in my dreams sometimes. It's dark and stirring, I think. Much more mature than my previous paintings. I asked him what he thought. He said it was pretty. I asked him if he liked the contrast between light and dark and if he noticed how I'd adjusted my brush strokes since my last painting and if it said anything to him. He just looked uncomfortable and repeated that it was pretty and took it away to be part of my next show. I really hate my keepers sometimes.

*

May 10

I asked if I could visit the garden next door. At first they said no, but I talked them into it. I promised to paint flowers and write songs and poems about flowers.

*

May 11

Flowers are so beautiful and soft and I can't even describe their smell. And no one ever goes into the garden! It's only there so that scientists can do research and tests. I picked a rose and brought it back with me. I snagged my thumb on a thorn while I was picking it. It was strange to see my blood. I didn't realize it was so very red. My thumb hurts a lot, but the rose was worth it. It's in a vase on my table. The vase was a present from another Artist. She works with glass. I'm glad that I have it. My rose is amazing. The petals are pale pink, almost translucent, but the middle of the rose is a warmer shade. I'm going to paint it. I'll do two, so I can send one to the woman who sent me the vase. I hope she likes it.

*

May 21

I can't get the poem right. There aren't words that can describe how wonderful flowers are to people who haven't seen them. I begged and begged, and they let me have a rosebush. It's in a pot. It doesn't have any flowers on it, but there are tiny buds that I think will be flowers soon. I read a bunch of articles about

how to take care of it. Maybe if I'm really good with the rose
bush and I keep it alive and healthy and I'm careful not to hurt
myself on its thorns, they'll let me have a kitten. I've never seen
one, but they seem nice. Now I have both my rosebush and the
angels to keep me company.

*

May 30

The buds are turning pink! The petals are starting to peek
out, and it's the most amazing thing I've ever seen. They don't
smell like flowers yet, but I do like the way the rosebush smells,
especially right after I water it.

I've been reading about bugs and pollination. I don't
know what I think of it. I almost wish that there were still bugs
instead of the machines that we have now, but at the same time,
the pictures of bugs are so creepy. I'm almost glad that they're
gone. That makes me feel guilty, but I don't know why.

*

June 2

It's blooming! It's the most beautiful thing ever! I have to
go paint it.

*

June 3

I asked for a kitten and they said yes! I'm having the best
week ever! I'm going to name it Marmalade.

*

June 5

They brought Marmalade yesterday. She's perfect and
tiny and fuzzy and warm. She's almost the same color as my
bronze angel's wings. When I picked her up, she started purring
and curled up into a little ball and rubbed her face against my
chin. I love her and she loves me and I'm not even close to alone
anymore.

*

96

June 15

Marmalade is so silly! She chases string and sunbeams and makes me laugh. She sleeps with me at night. At first it was weird having something else alive in my bed, moving around and sometimes stepping on my nose, but now I like it. It's really comforting, somehow.

*

June 18

Marmalade is sick. It's nothing serious, but she vomited all over my pillow in the middle of the night last night, and she hasn't been getting to her litter box. I woke up with her vomit in my hair, and I stepped in some of her poop. My keepers were doing a really good job of keeping the litter box clean so I didn't realize how terrible kitten poop is.

Marmalade had her vomit all through her fur, too. I cleaned her off with a warm washcloth before I showered. She looked so weak and miserable and sorry. I couldn't be mad, even when the smell of her vomit and poop make me gag and almost vomit myself. I've never vomited before—I'm pretty sure I don't want to ever, either.

My keepers wanted to take her away and get me a new, healthy kitten that would never vomit or poop on the floor, but I said no. I love Marmalade, disgusting vomit and poop and all.

*

July 4

I'm so happy, and it really is showing in my work. I'm getting so much done! I finished my flower poem, and I wrote one about kittens, too. The Artist who sent the vase wrote me a note thanking me for the painting, and she invited me to come and visit her, so I'm finally going to get to go somewhere. Her name is Catherine, and she promises that we'll be great friends.

*

July 27

Catherine is lots older than me, but she's nice. She made

me cocoa and toasted cheese sandwiches. I'd never seen anyone cook before. She told me that it makes her happy. She taught me a few things. Maybe I'll try cooking, too, when I'm older. I watched her blow glass. It was amazing. She made me a pink glass rose and we talked about art and the world and I told her about my bronze angel and she believed me. When I told her about Marmalade, she looked sad and said she'd had a puppy once. She told me stories about when she was my age and showed me her collection of motion pictures. They're so old! We watched one on this screen thing that she has. I liked it. The end was sad and it made me cry, but Catherine was crying too, and after that we had more cocoa and I can't wait to visit again.

*

August 5

I came to see Catherine again, and we talked a lot. She showed me her favorite glass piece. She's never showed it to anyone else before. She said that they wouldn't understand.

It's beautiful, but horrible somehow. At first glance, all you see are these beautiful ribbons of glass swirling around. Then, you realize that there's a figure inside, a glass woman. At least she looked like a woman to me. And she was trapped. The ribbons around her were her cage and she couldn't escape. I told Catherine that I knew how the woman felt, and Catherine hugged me and said that she did too and she was so glad to finally have someone who actually understood her work.

She told me about her first exhibition. They let her go, but she wishes that they hadn't. No one understood any of her work—no one felt anything at looking at it. They just thought it was pretty. The power was lost on them totally. And she said that everyone else in the building was wearing gray, and she'd insisted on wearing her favorite green dress, and everyone just stared at her like she was part of the exhibit. No one talked to her or asked her any questions about her work. They just stared blankly. She hated it.

*

August 7

Today Catherine and I are going to the museum. I should still be sleeping, but I woke up and I can't—I'm too excited.

*

August 8

I could spend every day at the museum and still not have enough time. How did I think I could be a real Artist? How can I compare my work with all of these great works? I feel like I've been calling rough sketches masterpieces. Catherine told me not to worry, that I am still young and I've got enough raw talent to fill an ocean, but I'm not sure. Am I really an Artist, or am I just a pale imitation who stands out because Art has been bred out of the rest of the population?

*

August 9

I asked Catherine why she thinks they made us while we were at the museum yesterday. If none of them understand the power and true beauty of art, why go through all the effort it must have taken to bring us back? Catherine thinks it's because Art and Artists are fashionable. It gives people who have enough money to buy our pieces bragging rights.

I'm worried about what will happen to us if the fashion changes. But at the same time, I'm sad for my keepers and all of the other people I haven't met, because I feel like they're all the same somehow. Like they're all dead inside. Sometimes I think it's a good thing that I don't know my keepers' names, because I'm afraid that even if I did I would still get them mixed up.

*

August 14

Marmalade died while I was with Catherine. They've already disposed of her body. They were surprised at how upset I am. They thought I knew she'd die. They said that kittens used to grow up into cats, and no one liked cats nearly as well, so kittens just die once they get too old now. But Marmalade wasn't too old. I wasn't going to stop loving her if she turned into a cat. I asked why they didn't just stop kittens from aging if no one wanted cats, and they said it wasn't possible. I hate them. They're stupid and callous and shallow and they don't even realize it. I think they might have just forgotten to feed Marmalade, even though they promised me that they'd remember.

I looked at my pillow, at the spot where she always slept, after they'd gone, and I started crying. I wish Catherine were here. She'd understand. This must have happened to her, too, with her puppy. I wish she'd warned me, but I guess she didn't want to make me unhappy any sooner than I needed to be.

Oh, Marmalade, I'm so sorry. If I'd known what they were going to do, I wouldn't have left you.

*

August 15

They brought another kitten, but it's stupid and gray and it isn't Marmalade and I just can't seem to stop crying.

*

August 16

I snuck out onto the roof again. The stupid new kitten tried to sleep with me in Marmalade's spot, and after that I knew I wouldn't be able to sleep.

Then, the most incredible thing happened. I was crying, and a hand touched my shoulder. I looked up, expecting it to be one of them about to yell at me for sneaking out and for crying about Marmalade, but it wasn't.

It was my bronze angel. He smiled at me. His face looked human— more human than the faces of my keepers do sometimes. His skin looked weathered, which makes sense, considering that angels fly around in all sorts of weather all of the time. His hair was short, and bronze, like his wings, and his eyes were the same deep green as the leaves on my rosebush. His hand was warm. His touch reminded me of Marmalade. I started telling him all about Marmalade and how much I missed her and how horrible the world was. As I cried, he picked me up and wrapped his wings around me. He rocked me back and forth.

Eventually, I stopped crying. I thought he was going to put me down, but instead, he whispered in a voice that sounded like Marmalade purring, "Hold on tight."

He jumped off of the side of the building. His arms were wrapped around me, and mine were twined around his neck, and even though I felt safe, I couldn't help gasping a little as we fell. Then his wings unfurled, and the wind caught us, and we were flying. His wings made great thumping sounds when he flapped them. We flew in circles, climbing higher into the sky. I could see the city spread out below me. The lights were beautiful. Then we were in a cloud. It was cold and wet and not at all how I'd imagined being inside a cloud would be. Then we were out, and I could see the stars. They took my breath away. I just stared as my angel flew. My eyes watered from the cold and the wind, but I refused to blink. I didn't think to question where we were going.

We didn't go back through any clouds on our way down. We landed in a field, next to a tiny house. Rows of wheat stretched as far as I could see in every direction.

I asked him if it was his home, and he said yes. We went inside and he made me cocoa, just like Catherine had, and I told him about my life. He told me a few things, too, about being an angel, but they're secrets. He did tell me that he'd been watching me for a while, just like I'd been watching him, and even though he wasn't supposed to talk to humans, he had decided to risk it to cheer me up. He had a cat—a full-grown cat—and she was nursing a litter of kittens. He promised that one of them would be my kitten, and I could come and visit it whenever I wanted, and he'd be sure to take good care of it so that someday it would be a cat, too, and maybe have kittens of its own. I picked a kitten with bronze and black patches, so that it would be like Marmalade, but not the same. I haven't named her yet.

I fell asleep at his house, and he brought me back and left me on the roof. I might have thought that the whole thing was a dream, but he left me a feather, tucked in my journal. Its ribbing is made out of metal, but the rest of the feather is soft and smooth, like Marmalade's fur.

*

August 26

I wrote Catherine and told her what happened. She's putting in a request for the two of us to live together. Then I can have my kitten at her house and she won't tell anyone when it grows up to be a cat. She asked me if I could ask the angel for a puppy for her, too. She's going to teach me how to cook and blow glass and I'm going to paint my angel. I think a painting of him would be real Art, like Catherine's woman trapped in the glass ribbon cage is real Art, because it'll come from my heart. And that really is what makes me different from my keepers, and probably all the rest of the people in the world. Except for Catherine and my Angel. We still feel things with our hearts.

~~~
~~~

About the Author

Jamie Lackey lives in Pittsburgh with her husband, author/game designer Paul Stefko, and their cat, Zuko. She earned her BA in Creative Writing from the University of Pittsburgh at Bradford, and her fiction has been appeared in dozens of venues, including *The Living Dead 2, Daily Science Fiction,* and *Beneath Ceaseless Skies.* She has also appeared on the Best Horror of the Year Honorable Mention and Tangent Online Recommended Reading Lists. She worked on the *Triangulation Annual Anthology Series* for four years, she reads slush for *Clarkesworld Magazine,* and is an assistant editor at *Electric Velocipede.*

She also enjoys reading, baking, traveling, and hiking, and she loves unicorns.